"Kate, you have my promise."

Ashington spoke in a gentle voice. "Whatever it is, I shall stand your friend and help you."

Katherine looked down at her love and knew that her feelings were not entirely unreciprocated. Could it be that he did love her and would understand?

"Please, my dear," Ashington coaxed with a smile. "Do you wish me to be thought the veriest bully for causing you to weep? It will do my reputation no good, you know."

His reputation! Katherine's hopes died stillborn. What a fool she had been to think, for even a moment, that she and Ashington might be together. If her secret came out, it would mean ruin for Ashington. He, who had been lionized by the ton, would be shunned by them if he married so far beneath him.

"I must go," she blurted, and drove her heels into her mount's flanks.

Ashington could only stare after her in amazement, and by the time he jumped back into his own saddle, she was gone.

Books by Elizabeth Michaels

HARLEQUIN REGENCY ROMANCE
17–TOLLIN'S DAUGHTER

THE FABRIC OF LOVE

ELIZABETH MICHAELS

Harlequin Books

TORONTO • NEW YORK • LONDON
AMSTERDAM • PARIS • SYDNEY • HAMBURG
STOCKHOLM • ATHENS • TOKYO • MILAN

"The fabric of my faithful love
No power shall dim or ravel . . ."

—Edna St. Vincent Millay

Published September 1991

ISBN 0-373-31158-3

THE FABRIC OF LOVE

CHAPTER ONE

THE TALL MAN REGARDED himself critically in the mirror. He touched a slender, elegant hand to his greying black hair, the enormous sapphire ring he wore on the index finger of that hand winking in the sunlight. The man frowned and ran his finger gently along the lines that stretched from nose to mouth; his blue eyes narrowed thoughtfully.

The other two men in the drawing room seemed unaware of their friend's self-scrutiny. They stood before the fireplace talking quietly and drinking brandy. One of the men looked at his watch and made a comment to his companion that made the man laugh aloud.

"Well?"

The two turned towards the door. "I say!" exclaimed one of them. "Look at you—look at her, Kes."

"I am, fool," said the man before the mirror. "My pet, you are a picture." He kissed his fingers.

Diantha, Countess of Blandford, did indeed look a picture. She stared haughtily at her guests, one hand toying with a quizzing glass, the other placed gracefully on her hip. Short red curls were brushed severely back from her forehead; her small frame was perfectly erect. A starched white neckcloth was tied round her throat in a casual Irlandaise, and highly polished top boots encased her trim calves. A blue frock coat and buff-coloured pantaloons completed her ensemble. In short, she looked every inch the slender gentleman of tender years and excellent birth.

Green eyes sparkling, Diantha swept Arthur, Lord Keswick, a deep bow. "A taking young buck, am I not?" She pirouetted before the gentlemen.

The third of the young men, who had remained silent until this point, said softly to Keswick, "You're wrong to encourage her in this, Kes. It's on your head if something goes wrong."

Lord Keswick shrugged. "Diantha was under no obligation to accept the wager, Ingham."

"That's right." Edwin Rankin nodded. "It's all in fun, you know."

Keswick closed his eyes for a moment, his expression pained. "You almost make me reconsider my position, Rankin," he murmured. "Almost!"

"That's quite enough," said Diantha. "If you wish to bait Rankin, Kes, you may go somewhere else to do it." She turned to Ingham. "If I wish to take Keswick's wager, 'tis my affair and none other's."

Ingham raised an eyebrow. "So?" he said. "Ashington will be most surprised to hear that."

There was a moment's silence. "I hadn't thought of Ashington," Rankin said, frankly worried. "He won't like this, Kes, you may be sure of that."

"Ashington need never learn of it," said Diantha uneasily. "After all, it's not as if I were going to Almack's like this. The only person who will see me, besides you three, will be this tailor whom Keswick bets me I can't fool."

"I stand by my wager, Di," said Keswick. "Despite the excellence of your disguise, there is no possibility that the man will not discern your...ah...feminine charms."

"We shall see, shan't we, Kes?" she said. "For myself, I am already planning what to do with my winnings. Five hundred pounds was the sum mentioned, was it not?"

"Come to think of it," said Edwin Rankin, "how will you pay her if she does win, Kes? Rumour has it that you're pockets-to-let; how will you raise the ready? And a monkey at that!"

Lord Keswick looked down at Rankin and spoke in a silkily threatening tone. "Rumour," he said, "can be a dangerous thing, my friend. Pray be most careful with it."

"No more," said Diantha flatly. "I have had quite enough of your bickering." She joined Keswick at the mirror to make one final adjustment to her neckcloth, then spread her arms wide. "Well, gentlemen?" she asked. "Shall I do?"

"Indeed you will," Edwin Rankin assured her. "Indeed you will!"

"And," added Lord Keswick, "though I don't expect to lose, either way, 'twill be the most amusing wager I've made in an age."

KATHERINE L'ECUSSON leaned her cheek against the cool glass of the window and blinked back sudden tears. There was nothing to cry about, she told herself firmly. No one, to the best of her knowledge, had ever actually died of boredom; only, perhaps, wished that they might. She sighed. It was not, she thought, as though there were not sufficient work to engage her. Maman and Henri were busy from dawn to dusk, while Katherine troubled herself with nothing more strenuous than a lending library novel or a particularly intricate piece of embroidery. She should be allowed to help out; she could be of use to them, and not allowing her to assist made it seem as though she weren't truly part of the family. She would tell them so, she decided, as soon as they came up to dinner.

Her heart lighter, Katherine lifted her face up to the sun and basked in its gentle warmth. The light brought a glow to her pale cheeks, and added a glossy finish to her heavy black hair. It was considerably longer than was the current fashion; all of London might rave about the Grecian mode and style its hair into a cap of short curls, but Katherine still preferred to let hers hang straight down her back. The long hair and the clarity of her blue eyes made her look younger than her twenty years, and the simplicity of the high-waisted muslin gown she wore did nothing to dispel the illusion.

The sun went behind a cloud, and Katherine idly began to watch the traffic in the street below. Her attention was captured by four young gentlemen leaving the shop; she pressed her face against the glass to get a better look at them. The one in the centre of the group, a fiery redhead, caught her eye as he swaggered boastfully along. Katherine frowned and tried to think what it was about the young man that seemed wrong. Perhaps it was the exaggerated roll of the youth's hips? Then she saw another gentleman approaching the group and forgot all about the young red-haired gentleman. She pushed the window open and thrust her head through the opening, peering intently down into the street.

"Katherine, *ma petite,* what are you doing?" The tiny silver-haired woman shook her head as she hurried into the sitting room. "It is not *convenable* to hang out the window. A young lady does not behave so."

Katherine blushed hotly and slammed the window shut. "What?" she said. "I . . . I did not hear you, Maman."

"I said," the lady repeated, gently taking her daughter's sleeve and pulling her away from the window, "that a lady does not stare out the window. Is this not so?"

Katherine opened her mouth to argue, then closed it again. She waited until her mother had settled with a sigh onto the divan, then said, "Maman?"

"Yes, *chérie?*" Marie L'Ecusson's eyes were closed; she spoke without opening them.

Katherine took a deep breath. "I wish to begin working in the shop," she said.

Marie's eyes flew open. *"Non, non, non,"* she said. "We have been all over this, Katherine, a dozen times or more. A lady does not—"

"Lady?" Katherine clenched her fists. "Maman, I am no lady, and you know it!" she cried. "My brother is a tradesman, as was my father before him. No matter how much you seclude me, or how well brought up I am, I am no more than a shopkeeper's daughter."

"You are not!" Marie was fierce. "You are a lady born, and never let me hear you say otherwise. Your brother and I, and your papa, God rest his soul, have done what we must to support ourselves and I am not ashamed of that. But you, Katherine, you are the hope of our family."

"A lady born?" Katherine spluttered. "Maman, how can you be so obtuse? Is this my manor, then?" she demanded, gesturing about her. Her outstretched arms indicated the small sitting room, the bedchambers and the cramped kitchen. The rooms were comfortable and tastefully appointed; it was, nonetheless, just a small flat above a shop. "What is my brother's title, then? Lord Seamster? The Marquis of Thread?"

"Katherine!" Her mother seemed close to tears.

Katherine bit her lip. "Maman, I'm sorry," she said. "This temper of mine..."

Henri L'Ecusson entered the sitting room and dropped down beside his mother gratefully. He was very like his sister in looks, though a bit broader in frame. He shared Katherine's height, her black hair and her honest blue eyes. Henri was dressed quietly but tastefully, as became one who was fast becoming the most sought-after tailor in London. Just at the moment, he was smiling quietly to himself, mightily amused by something. "What are you sorry for now?" he asked his sister.

"It is of no moment," said Marie. She hugged her daughter tightly. "A bagatelle, eh, *ma douce?*" Marie turned to her son. "Was your business profitable, Henri?" she asked.

"Indeed it was." He nodded. "A blue twill redingote for Monsieur Ingham, a frock coat—" his mouth twitched "—for Ingham's little friend, and an evening coat and breeches for Monsieur Rankin."

Marie snorted. "Rankin! Now there we have a prime example of English manhood.... A greater fool never lived."

Henri burst out laughing. "Surely you're being a little harsh, Maman? And his money is good, *non?*" He winked at his sister. "Besides, Edwin Rankin is not the greatest fool in London. Why, he's not even the greatest fool to have passed through our doors."

"But how can that be?" Marie said. "No one could possibly be more empty-headed than Monsieur Rankin. Such a creature would be too stupid to live."

"I can think of such a person," said Henri, digging a coin out of his pocket and sticking it into his screwed-up eye. Tilting his head back, he said in a high-pitched voice, teeth clenched, "I say, though, Henri, don't you think these shoulders could stand a bit more padding? Mean to say, don't want to appear underendowed, eh, old boy?" He stalked across the room, back stiff, and ogled Katherine owlishly. "Now there's a bit of all right. A devilish pretty girl, what?"

Katherine could not help but laugh, and Marie bit her lip, trying to hide her smile. "You should not belittle such a good customer as Monsieur Basingstoke, my son. We have, after all, done a great deal of work for him."

"Yes; what a pity that he hasn't paid for it," said Henri. "Seriously, Maman, I don't understand why you insist that we extend credit to Basingstoke. He's already so deeply in our debt that he could never hope to pay us off."

Marie waggled her head. "Ah, Henri, there are reasons and reasons," she said obscurely. "And you forget, *mon cher,* that Monsieur Basingstoke has done us one service for which we may never repay him."

"And what might that be?" Henri asked.

"He brought Lord Ashington to us," said Marie.

"True." Henri was bound to admit.

"So?" said Katherine. Neither Marie nor Henri noticed her heightened colour. "What is so important about his lordship?"

"It was not until Ashington took us up that we really became à la mode," Henri explained to his sister. "He is all that is most admired in Polite Society...a pink of the ton and member of the Four Horse Club, well-born, well-raised, and extremely well-heeled. In short, sister, Ashington is a prime gun, slap up to the mark and awake upon all suits. What he does, all others copy." He smiled. "Including," he added, "patronizing a small but exclusive tailor shop intriguingly named L'Ecusson." Henri turned to his mother. "Your point is well taken, Maman. As long as Basingstoke and Ashington are such good friends, I suppose that it does behoove us not to press the moronic Freddy too hard for payment."

"Exactly," said Marie, and surprised Katherine and Henri by laughing aloud for no discernable reason. "Never fear, *mes enfants*. Monsieur Basingstoke will pay his debt to us in full, and even, perhaps, a little over."

DIANTHA CLOSED THE DOOR behind her and stopped for a moment to grin triumphantly at her friends. The shop she had just left was a small one; the windows were discreetly covered, with only a roll of tastefully figured velvet displayed to entice the discriminating passerby. The sign over the door was inscribed, simply, L'Ecusson.

Edwin Rankin could barely contain his excitement. "You did it, Di, you did it," he chortled. "The man never even suspected. 'Pon my word, he did not."

Diantha turned to Lord Keswick. "Well, Kes?" she asked. "Do you agree? Did I hoax him?"

"There was one moment when I thought he knew," the tall man said, then shrugged. "But I suppose not. He would surely have spoken if he had." It was Keswick's turn to bow to Diantha. "You've won the wager fair and square, Di, more's the pity. I'll send the money over in the morning."

Diantha spoke softly. "If you'd rather I waited, Kes..."

Lord Keswick flushed. "Save your charity, Diantha, for those in need of it. I, you may be assured, am not."

Diantha rolled her eyes. "Pray forgive me, my lord," she said in a boy's gruff tones. "I'd no wish to offend you, my lord."

"Perhaps you should call her, or should I say *him* out," suggested Rankin gleefully. "'Twould make for a most intriguing match."

"So it would." The deep voice made Diantha gasp. The four turned as one to regard the man who stood, smiling sardonically, behind them.

"Ash!" stammered Diantha. "I—I..."

"Well met, gentlemen," said Thomas Blythe, Lord Ashington, bending his head ever so slightly. He looked the group over lazily and raised an eyebrow at Ingham. The man coloured.

"Good day, Ashington," said Lord Keswick imperturbably. "Back in Town so soon? How was your trip?"

Edwin Rankin had gone white at the sight of Ashington. "This wasn't my idea, Ashington," he squeaked. "I tried to tell her it was wrong. I did!"

"Oh, shut up, Edwin," said Ingham in disgust.

Ashington stared at Rankin contemptuously, then turned his attention pointedly elsewhere. "Well, Diantha?" he said pleasantly, his brown eyes boring down into hers. "Whose notion was this?" He indicated her attire.

"Ash, I . . ." she began. "I . . ."

"Yes," he remarked. "You said that already." He turned to Keswick. "Can you shed any light on this matter, Keswick?" The tall man stared back at Ashington without speaking. "No? Well, I believe that Diantha and I shall say goodbye, then. Goodbye!" He took the woman's arm and steered her firmly away from the group.

They walked in silence for some minutes. The streets were relatively empty; the late afternoon sun gilded the cobblestones and cast long shadows before them. Diantha looked up at Ashington out of the corner of her eye and thought complacently that he was still the most handsome man she had ever seen. The combination of warm brown eyes, brown hair that curled boyishly over the back of his collar and skin weathered by days spent outdoors hunting and riding was difficult to resist. Diantha saw two women eyeing

Ashington and took his arm possessively, only to jump away when she remembered that she was still dressed as a boy. "You aren't angry with me, are you, Ash?" she asked.

"Angry?" he said. "No, Di, I'm not angry."

She breathed a gusty sigh of relief. "I'm so glad," she exclaimed, and gave Ashington's arm a quick squeeze. "Oh, Ash, it was such fun. He measured me for a suit and never even suspected. The man never even suspected!"

"I wouldn't be so sure of that, if I were you," Ashington said. "He'd have to be a fool not to have known. I've dealt with this Henri, Diantha. He's no fool."

"Oh, pooh!" Diantha dismissed the tailor with a wave. "He's just a little shopkeeper; what does he know? And Ash! You'll never guess how much money I won."

Ashington laughed ruefully. "A wager! I might have known it."

"A monkey...isn't that famous? Five hundred pounds! Keswick was furious."

"You won money from Keswick? You'll be lucky if you ever collect it." The pair turned down Green Street and climbed the stairs of number twelve. Ashington motioned Diantha's butler away as he opened the door for them; the servant was too accustomed to his mistress's fits and starts to betray any surprise at her unusual attire. The peer kept a firm grip on Diantha's arm and guided her up the stairs and into the drawing-room.

"That's not fair, Ash," said Diantha reproachfully. "I know you're not excessively fond of Keswick, but even you must admit that he always pays his wagers." She stretched, then sidled up to Ashington and put her arms round him. "Have you missed me?" she asked. "You've been gone a whole week; did you bring me a present?" Her eyes glittered.

Ashington took a square velvet box out of his breast pocket. He turned away as Diantha opened it.

"Oh!" she gasped. "Oh!" A magnificent diamond parure lay nestled in the large box: necklace, cuffs and earbobs. "Oh, my dear," she said, then stopped. She looked blank. "But... Ash, this isn't..."

"It's over, Di," he said flatly. "We're finished."

"But you said you weren't angry," Diantha protested.

"I'm not," said Ashington. "We've had a good run, you and I. I've enjoyed your company immensely."

"My company!" Diantha exploded. "I shouldn't need to remind you that you've enjoyed a great deal more than my company, my lord."

Ashington closed his eyes for a moment and sighed. "Diantha, must we be unkind to each other?" he asked. "I was not your first lover and I beg leave to doubt that I'll be your last. Why make a fuss?"

"Just tell me why, Ash. Why?"

"You've become a shade too wild for me, my pet," he said reluctantly. "I suspect that you'd be happier with a gentleman more lively than myself."

"But that's not true," Diantha began. "I—"

"Don't," said Ashington sharply. "It won't do either of us any good."

Diantha threw the box to the floor and planted her hands on her hips. "I'm not some little nobody you can throw over whenever it suits you," she hissed. "Need I remind you that my papa was a duke and my late husband an earl? My godfather is the Prince Regent himself! I'm better born than you are, Ashington. I could make London very uncomfortable for you, if I told people how you'd treated me."

Ashington laughed, and Diantha clenched her fists in rage. "Stop and think, Di, before you begin talking, who it is that will be most hurt by the gossip," he warned her. "It won't be me." He took her face between strong fingers and said gently, "Can't you be content to part as friends, my dear? I shall always treasure the memory of our time together."

Diantha clung to him. "I'll change, Ash, I swear I will," she said tearfully. "Just give me a chance."

"But I shouldn't want you to change," he said, swiftly disengaging himself. "You are charming just as you are. And there will be no end of gentlemen clamouring to tell you so, wait and see." Ashington took up his hat and cane. "Goodbye, Diantha," he said, and was gone.

Diantha, Countess of Blandford, wiped her face and slowly, sadly, bent down to pick up the jewellery that had spilled across the floor.

CHAPTER TWO

MARIE L'ECUSSON SEWED the last stitch in the hem of a blue superfine frock coat and neatly cut the thread. "Done!" she said aloud and set the coat aside to be pressed. She did not move; leaning her head against the back of the workroom chair, she closed her eyes and listened to her children talking in the next room.

"How foolish you are, little sister," Henri said. "Did you really think that Maman would let you work in the shop, after all the times you've asked and all the times she has said no?"

"Not really," Katherine confessed. "I just thought ... I just felt so ..."

"So what, *ma soeur?* Tell me," Henri coaxed.

Marie could hear the rustle of Katherine's skirts as the girl rose and began to stride back and forth across the sitting room. "I felt as if I were suffocating," Katherine said. "Henri, you cannot know how awful it is for me sometimes, sitting in this room until I think I shall go mad. I watch the people in the street outside, and listen to the gentlemen's voices drifting up from the shop and wonder if I shall ever go anywhere or do anything."

"You exaggerate, Kate," Henri said, a note of reproach in his voice. "You do go out from time to time; Maman gives a great deal of thought to your amusement, you know."

"I know she does. And I am grateful for it, truly, Henri. But trips to Astley's Amphitheatre and sedate walks in Green Park do little to relieve the tedium."

"She is quite right, though, to refuse to allow you to work in the shop. It would not be at all the thing."

"Oh, yes, it would be much more the thing," Katherine snapped, "for me to waste the rest of my life in these rooms!"

Henri laughed. "Now, there you go too far, my pet. However aged you may feel, I promise you that you have a year or two left before you are quite sunk in your dotage."

Katherine sighed gustily. "I know, I know," she said. "And it is quite dreadful of me to sit here and complain, when there are so many people who have so much more to complain of than I. I simply wonder, sometimes . . . what will become of me?"

"If you could choose, Kate, what kind of life would you wish for yourself?" Henri asked.

In the next room, Marie leaned forward in her chair, listening intently.

"Oh, an ordinary sort of life, I suppose," Katherine replied. "I should like to marry, of course, and have children. But not just any man will do, you understand; my gentleman will be someone very special.

He will be strong and loving and have a wonderful sense of humour."

Marie smiled and chuckled softly with satisfaction.

"A paragon among men, to be sure," Henri said. "And where would one find such perfection?"

"You may tease me, Henri, but you will not shake my faith," Katherine said in a dreamy voice. "I know that he exists somewhere. I can almost see him, sometimes, in my mind. And he is waiting for me; I truly believe that. Though he is tall and handsome and many ladies look at him longingly, he is waiting only for me."

"I think sometimes, too, of the lady who will be my bride," Henri said. "She will be small and full of life—a firebrand, to be exact. A lady of beauty and grace, but no pretence; not for me your milk-and-water misses with die-away airs! My lady will be..." He stopped.

"She will be...?" Katherine prompted him.

"This is foolishness," he said abruptly. "It is all very well to dream, but one must face reality, Katherine. Such a life is not for me, nor for you, either."

"But—"

"You, my dear Kate, will be lucky indeed if you can marry a tradesman of means, who will see to your needs and not work you too hard," Henri said roughly.

Marie was compelled to clap a hand over her mouth to keep from crying out in dismay.

"And for me," Henri continued, "a strong woman, who will give me sons and toil beside me in the shop, when Maman is no longer able to assist me."

"Oh, Henri," Katherine whispered.

"And why not?" Henri said loudly. "Why should we think ourselves so much better than those around us? Maman may call you a lady and worry me about my speech and deportment, but Maman is just...well, Maman! We are tradesmen, *chérie,* no better or worse than the greengrocer next door or the milliner across the way. Put away your dreams, Kate; dreams are for children." The door slammed behind Henri, and Marie heard her son stamp down the stairs to the shop.

Marie nodded her head slowly. *You know you are different, my children, don't you?* she thought. *You know you were not meant for such a life as this. But trust me,* mes enfants: *I have not schemed and planned all these years for naught. I shall show you the life you were meant to lead,* Marie vowed silently, *or die trying.*

LORD KESWICK STRETCHED long legs out before him, and yawned behind a discreetly upraised hand. "I don't know why you keep saying that Ashington can't do this to you," he said. "He has done it."

The Countess of Blandford pointed her finger at Keswick. "I hold you responsible for this, Kes," she said. "If it hadn't been for that cursed wager—"

"Untrue, Diantha," responded his lordship. "Ashington had begun to tire of you long before this happened. Did you not yourself tell us that he has been conspicuous by his absence of late? I daresay the wager was in the nature of a last straw.''

''It infuriates me,'' said Diantha from between clenched teeth, ''that you are taking all this so calmly.''

''My dear Diantha, can you be so naïve as to imagine that I care, one way or another?'' Keswick asked, one brow raised in astonishment.

Diantha took on a wounded expression. ''I thought you were my friend?''

Keswick shrugged. ''I am,'' he said. ''And while we are on the subject,'' he added, meeting her gaze steadily, ''I would not be loath to be more than a friend to you.''

''Kes!'' gasped Diantha.

''You needn't look so shocked, Di. You know I've always found you most attractive. Why not a liaison between us? I promise you, you'll find me to be every bit as generous as Ashington.'' Keswick watched Diantha without moving. ''Ah, I see that your answer is no,'' he said dispassionately. ''You might wish to reconsider, my dear. I think you'll find yourself a trifle lonely without Ashington's company.''

''It's not that I'm not flattered,'' Diantha said, eyeing Keswick warily. ''And, under other circumstances, who can say?''

''You needn't look as though you're afraid I'll bite you,'' Keswick said. ''A personable gentleman has far too many opportunities to be upset by one refusal.''

"I suppose I should be insulted by that," said Diantha, looking as though she were well on her way to that very emotion.

"If I am not, then why should you be?" asked Keswick. There appeared to be no answer to that question, so Diantha wisely held her tongue. "Besides," Keswick went on, "I should like to hear what these circumstances are."

Diantha dropped to her knees before the peer. "First, promise me that you won't laugh?"

"The last time I laughed aloud was in infancy," drawled Keswick. "Life is too, too tiresome to waste one's energies guffawing."

"I think," Diantha said, her eyes on his face, "that it would be a very good thing if Ashington and I were to wed."

Keswick stared at the young woman for a long moment, then his mouth opened and peals of laughter escaped him.

Diantha leapt to her feet. "I despise you," she hissed, red-faced. "I despise you!"

Keswick had regained control of himself. "No wonder Ashington threw you over," he said. "You're excessively unattractive when you're angry." He held up a hand as she stamped her foot and looked wildly round the room for something to throw. "Control yourself, my dear countess," he told her. "You're quite right; I shouldn't have laughed. I was simply taken by surprise."

Diantha wavered for a moment, then said stiffly, "I accept your apology." She moved to the bell pull and asked, "Shall I ring for your hat and cane?"

Keswick didn't move. "Don't sulk, my dear, it doesn't become you," he said. "Tell me more about this notion of yours. What makes you imagine that you and Ashington should suit, putting aside the fact that he refuses to have anything more to do with you?"

Diantha was taken aback. "Why, of course we should suit," she said. "We know each other so well."

"You know each other as man and mistress," Keswick pointed out. "Ashington's so infernally top-lofty, I don't believe that he'd be content with—"

"Be very careful what you say, Kes," Diantha warned him.

"A woman of experience, shall we say?" Keswick finished smoothly. "A tongue-tied virgin would be more his style."

"I doubt it," Diantha said. "He's too easily bored to be happy with some milk-and-water miss. No, he's angry with me now, but once he cools off, he'll miss me, you'll see. I shall make sure of that. And then..." She paused, adding softly, "I do love him, you know."

"The more fool you," said Keswick, coming suddenly to his feet. "I'd never have thought to hear such pap from you, Diantha. I had thought you a woman of sense."

"How can you, Kes?" Diantha blinked back tears.

"Don't play the injured fawn with me," said his lordship curtly. "It won't wash; I know your true nature too well. I shall see myself out, thank you." He turned at the doorway for one parting shot. "I shall be watching the papers with breathless anticipation. I hope to be the first to felicitate you upon your betrothal." The sound of his laughter echoed back to Diantha as he left the room.

"Damn you, Arthur Keswick," she whispered fiercely. "I will have Ashington. I will!"

THE MAN ON THE PEDESTAL was tall, so tall that he could not see the reflection of his head in the specially made mirror before him. He was also exceedingly thin; though he approached six and one-half feet in height, his weight was less than fourteen stone. The overall effect was that of an elongated stork, a resemblance which increased when he tipped his head to one side to regard his image.

The door behind the man opened. Without looking, the man said in a ridiculously high-pitched voice, "I say, Henri, this just won't do! This frock coat is too...too... Well, just too dashed *too,* if you know what I mean."

"I am most sorry that monsieur is not pleased by our work," came a quiet voice.

Frederick Basingstoke whirled about so quickly that the monocle flew out of his eye. "Who the dev... That is to say, who are you? And where's Henri?"

"I am Henri's maman," said Marie calmly. She crossed the room to sit in a chair that stood beside the mirror. Mr. Basingstoke followed her progress by turning his body, mouth agape.

"But what are you doing here? Where's Henri?" he asked again. "It isn't proper for you to be here alone with me."

Marie laughed. "My dear sir, I am nearly old enough to be your mother," she said. "I believe that both of our reputations will survive a few moments' private conversation. There is a matter that I wish to discuss with you."

"If it's about my bill, you may rest assured that I—"

Marie held up a hand. "It is about your bill, but only indirectly," she said. "How would you like to be quit of all financial responsibility to us?"

"I should dashed well love it," he admitted. "I can't recall quite what I owe you, but it must be—" he paused warily "—a hundred pounds or so?"

"Seven times that amount," said Marie.

Basingstoke's pale blue eyes bulged. "Seven hundred pounds?" he shrilled. "That can't be right. You must have overcharged me!"

Marie remained calm. "I have receipts to prove it," she said. "I have documented your expenditures most carefully."

In his agitation, the man jumped down from the pedestal and began to stride round the room, scattering pins from his unfinished frock coat with every step. "Well, I don't have it," he said. "You may do what you will, but I'm pockets-to-let, and that's the truth of the matter."

"Ah, but I have not asked you for money, have I?" Marie said. "Although, if you were unable to fulfil my request, I might find myself forced to set the bailiffs on you."

Basingstoke stopped pacing and stared down at the seated woman. "Are you trying to blackmail me?" he asked incredulously. "Because if you are, you're wasting your time. There's nothing to blackmail me with and no one to care even if there were." He thought for a moment, then said, "Except for my aunt. And you'd have a dashed time of it trying to make her understand whatever it is you think I've done, which I haven't, of course." He stopped again, then sank down onto the pedestal. "I'm confused," he said.

Marie chuckled. "I'm not trying to blackmail you...exactly," she said. "Just think of it as a favour for a favour. You fulfil my request and your bill is forgotten." She eyed him speculatively, then added, "And any future bills, as well."

Basingstoke perked up a bit. He retrieved his dangling monocle and stuck it back into his eye. "Any future bills as well?" he said. "Hmmm...what's the favour?"

Marie raised her chin proudly. "I wish you to bring my daughter out," she said.

"What?" he asked stupidly.

"I wish you to present my daughter to the ton."

Once again the monocle abruptly left the man's eye socket, to swing gently back and forth at the end of the string attached to his waistcoat. "You must be mad," he said. "That's it...you're not really Henri's mother, you're just some madwoman, wandered in off the street." He fumbled in his pocket for a coin. "Here, take this and be on your way. Go ahead, take it."

Marie stared at his outstretched hand silently until finally he let it fall. "I assure you, monsieur, I am no madwoman," she said. "Though I do understand your feelings, I promise you. You think my Katherine to be some little shopgirl, low born and ill bred, with no more idea of the social graces than a street urchin. That is not the case."

"But it's impossible," Basingstoke said. "Impossible!"

Marie rose slowly to her feet. "Very well, then, monsieur," she said mournfully, "I take it that we may expect payment of your bill today, then?"

"No, dash it all," spluttered the man. "I told you, I don't have the money!"

"How unfortunate," said Marie. "It must be the bailiffs, then."

"You can't be serious," he protested.

"Monsieur, of one thing you may be sure: I am deadly serious," said Marie. Basingstoke looked into her face for a moment and was convinced.

"Tell me more about your daughter," he said.

Marie smiled and sat down again. "First," she said, "I believe that I shall tell you a little about myself. I was born in France," she began.

"I come of an old and quite illustrious family; my father was the Comte de Berceau." She chuckled. "You needn't look so sceptical, monsieur. I promise you, I should have no difficulty in proving it to you, and will, if you so desire. At any rate, my father knew long before the Troubles began that all was not well in France. He would never have thought of sending any of my five brothers out of the country, for it was their duty and their honour to stand beside him. But I was his only daughter; he could not bear the thought that I should be in danger, even for a moment. So he sent me to England with my governess, for what he called a long vacation, when I was seventeen years old." She stared sightlessly off into space, her face suddenly old and lined. "At first, all was well. I received letters regularly from Papa and all my brothers, and my governess was sent more than sufficient funds for my needs. Then, as the situation in France worsened, the letters began to grow more and more infrequent and finally stopped completely. I was frantic with worry and mad to return to France, but my governess would not allow it. My papa had been very wise, you see; he had made Hélène, my governess, swear an oath that she would keep me in England until he himself, or one of my brothers, came to take me home. So we waited, and waited, and waited. Gradually, I came to realize that no one would be coming for me, that they must all be dead."

"Madame, you needn't—"

"It was like being in hell," Marie said simply. "I was devastated by my grief and my guilt. I truly believe that if it had not been for Hélène, I would have died myself. Then the cruellest blow of all befell me; my Hélène was struck and killed by a drunken young gentleman in a curricle."

"Good Lord," said Basingstoke faintly.

"Oh, monsieur, the Lord was not good that day," said Marie sadly, then she smiled. "Or perhaps He was, for it was then, in my darkest hour, that I met Henry, who was to be my husband."

The tall man looked horrified. "Not the man in the curricle?"

"Not the driver, no," said Marie. "A...bystander, one might say."

"I take it he was a tradesman?" said Basingstoke. It was Marie's turn to look horrified.

"Oh, no, he was a gentleman," she said. "The younger son of a viscount, in fact."

"Then why...how...?" Basingstoke looked round the tailor shop.

Marie shrugged. "To Henry, I was the woman whom he loved and the daughter of a comte, but to his family I was simply a penniless French nothing," she explained. "They told him that if we were wed, they would cut him off without a cent. They were as good as their word."

"I see," said Frederick Basingstoke inanely.

"So, monsieur, my daughter is entitled to a come-out," said Marie, "and I am determined that she will have it." She looked fierce. "I have worked and saved since the day of her birth to make it possible. Will you be the one to ruin my plans, my dreams?"

Basingstoke spread his hands. "But, madame!" he said. "Why me? Would not her father's family be better suited to sponsor her? Who are they, by the way?"

"Who they are is of no moment," said Marie. "When they turned their backs on Henry and me, I turned my back on them. We shall not discuss them. As to why you . . ." She smiled again. "Do you recall your Great-Aunt Lucinda?"

"Not really," he said, "she married a Frenchman and moved to . . ." Basingstoke looked thunder-struck.

"Just so," nodded Marie. "Your Great-Aunt Lucinda was my Tante Lucinda. So what was more natural than that I should approach you, kinsman as you are?"

"And debtor," put in Basingstoke dryly.

"True," Marie said. "But be honest with me, monsieur. Would you have even listened to my tale, had I not forced you?"

"Probably not," he admitted. He sat for a moment, his brow wrinkled in thought. "You wouldn't really set the bailiffs on me, would you?"

"I would," she said. "With great reluctance, but I would."

"Very well, then," he said with a sigh. "It appears that I have no choice but to sponsor my cousin."

Marie clapped her hands. *"Très bien!"* she said. "Thank you, *mon ami*. You will never regret this." She rose to her feet again. "I shall contact you after I have broken the news to Katherine. You needn't worry, monsieur, for I have planned this very carefully." She turned back at the doorway for a final word. "By the way, you are quite right about the coat. It is a little too... *too!*" She smiled and was gone.

Frederick Basingstoke sat on the pedestal for a long time after Marie had left, shaking his head, before he finally retrieved his monocle and screwed it back into place.

CHAPTER THREE

KATHERINE LOOKED WARILY about the marble and gilt foyer as Frederick Basingstoke set down her portmanteau.

"Here we are," he said. "You needn't look daggers at me, Miss L'Ecusson. This wasn't my idea, you know."

"I am perfectly well aware of that fact, Mr. Basingstoke," she said stiffly.

He held up a hand. "You must call me Freddy," he said. "And I shall call you Kate; we are cousins of some sort, are we not?" Katherine ground her teeth as he went on blithely, "And here is Aunt Honoria. Good day, Aunt! I have brought Katherine L'Ecusson to you, just as I promised. Won't you make her welcome?" Under his breath, he muttered to Katherine, "Don't pay any mind if she seems a bit... confused."

The lady descending the stairs had reached that point in life often referred to as "a certain age." This fact did not appear to trouble her; indeed, she seemed wonderfully unburdened by any heaviness of mind as she floated down towards them, singing softly to herself, trailing a beautiful silk shawl behind her.

"Aunt Honoria," said Freddy more loudly. "Here is Cousin Katherine, come to stay with us. Will you say good day to her?"

"Of course I shall, Freddy," said Lady Honoria Basingstoke calmly, pushing a mass of grey hair back off her face. "There's no need to shout." She came up to Katherine and stood so close that Katherine stepped back in alarm. Honoria peered up into her face and pronounced definitely, "Well, she may be tall, but she doesn't look anything like Lucinda."

"Now, Honoria . . ." began Freddy.

"I see that as a virtue," Honoria continued, ignoring her nephew. "My Aunt Lucinda was an enormous, horselike creature. Every time she'd bend down to kiss me, I quite expected her to whinny."

"Aunt Honoria," said Freddy reproachfully.

"Of course, her French suitor did seem to prefer her that way," Honoria mused. "He'd stand before her, a tiny little man, and clasp his hands and murmur, *'Très grande! Très grande!'* And he must have liked her size, mustn't he, for he did marry her. There was great rejoicing in the house that day, I can tell you! My poor grandparents had despaired of ever marrying her off, and she ended up wed to a French lord, no less." Honoria shook her head, scattering hairpins far and wide. "It just goes to show you, though, doesn't it. It takes all kinds."

"Indeed it does," said Freddy, rolling his eyes eloquently in Katherine's direction.

Honoria blinked. "What were we talking about?" she asked no one in particular.

"We were greeting Cousin Katherine, Aunt, who has lately arrived from France," said her nephew patiently. "Remember?"

"Of course I do, Freddy, I'm not a fool," retorted Honoria. She held out a hand to Katherine, accompanied by a smile of dazzling brilliance. "Welcome my child. How very happy we are that you've come. Was your trip strenuous?"

"Not at all, Lady Basingstoke," answered Katherine.

"But you must call me Aunt, my dear," said Honoria, still holding Katherine's hand. "It should make me feel quite ancient to be called 'Lady' by such a young and pretty thing."

"As you wish . . . Aunt," Katherine said shyly. She squeezed Honoria's hand. "You are very good to have me," she added, and for that moment, at least, meant it.

Katherine had been surprised, but not too surprised, by her mother's revelations. After all the years of hearing Marie tell her that she was a lady, and the hope of her family, the news of her mother's background had not come as a very great shock. What had stunned her was her mother's plan for her come-out. She had railed and wept, begged and refused outright, but to no avail; Marie was dead set on this plan of hers and nothing Katherine could say had swayed her in the least.

"Are you a merry creature, my dear?" asked Honoria. "You have the eyes of a girl who likes to laugh, but you don't look very happy at the moment." Honoria stepped close to Katherine again. This time, Katherine bore her scrutiny unflinchingly. "You have the look of someone I know," she said.

"Perhaps Great-Aunt Lucinda?" suggested her nephew.

"Don't be a dolt, Freddy," Honoria advised him sharply. "I've already told you that she doesn't look like Lucinda. No, it's someone else. Who was your father, girl? He was English, was he not?"

Katherine blushed. This was a question that she herself would like an answer to! Marie had steadfastly refused to discuss Katherine's father with her. All she had said was that he was the younger son of a viscount and that his family had turned his back on them when he and Marie had wed.

"You wouldn't have known him, Aunt," Freddy said hastily. "He was . . . somewhat reclusive."

"He wasn't all about in his head, was he?" asked Honoria. "It would certainly hurt the girl's chances to have a madman for a father." Freddy could not quite contain a small choke of laughter. Honoria said calmly, "Oh, but it's all right for me to be mad, Freddy. I am an old woman, with my own fortune. I don't need anything from anyone; quite the contrary, in fact. I keep you dancing to my tune by carefully doling out money, a dribble at a time, just to keep you interested, so to speak." She patted her nephew's cheek affectionately. "Though I daresay you might stay around even if I were destitute. What do you think, nevvy?"

Freddy kissed her on the forehead and said, "I think that you are an awful old thing, Aunt. But you'll do your best for Kate, won't you? Chaperon her, I mean, and perhaps throw a ball in her honour?"

"I have more than ample funds to defray your expenses," said Katherine. "Maman said..."

"You keep your money for your clothing and such," said Honoria. She surveyed Katherine's neat brown twill redingote and morning dress and added, "You will need a whole new wardrobe and that won't come cheaply." Katherine ground her teeth at this calm dismissal of her new outfit, but held her peace as Honoria went on, "No, I shall see to the ball myself. It's been an age since I did an entertainment. 'Twill afford me a world of pleasure to decide exactly whom I shall not invite." She pushed a hand through her hair and murmured, "Perhaps my cousin Sefton would like to help me decide."

Katherine's eyes widened. "Lady Sefton?" she asked Freddy. "Patroness of Almack's?"

"Actually Lord Sefton, her husband," Freddy told her smugly. "You'll have no difficulty with vouchers to Almack's, cos. The Patronesses may play their little games with other debutantes, picking and choosing whom to admit, but you needn't give it another thought. Kate, you are in for the time of your life!"

Katherine could not help but be impressed. So essential was an entrée to Almack's Assembly Rooms for any young lady about Town that the place was often referred to sarcastically as the Marriage Mart. And that was, after all, the purpose of all Marie's schemes and machinations: to find Katherine a husband, a well-born and, presumably, rich husband. Katherine tried to stifle a spasm of bitterness. However much she tried not to think of it, however positive a state of mind she might try to cultivate, there were times when she could not help but feel like a prize cow, on the block and up for auction!

"MY LORD ASHINGTON, SIR."

"See him in, Croaker." Frederick Basingstoke breathed lightly on his monocle, then began to polish it gently with a lawn handkerchief. He frowned at the lens, picked at an invisible spot with a beautifully kempt nail, then continued to rub.

"Still playing with that toy of yours, I see," said Ashington. "What a damned silly affectation."

"'Lo, Ash," said his friend, not lifting his eyes from his task. "Make yourself comfortable. Brandy's on the table." He examined his work. "I fail to see the difference between this—" he waved the monocle "—and an ordinary quizzing glass. Why does the one so offend you and the other not?"

Ashington helped himself to the brandy, pulled an armchair a little closer to the fire and sat down. "Quite simple, Freddy. The quizzing glass is as ubiquitous as the air we breathe. Everyone has one, so they're virtually invisible. That thing, by reason of its sheer singularity, is always intruding itself upon one's notice."

"Do go on, Ash," said a pleased Freddy. "That's quite the nicest thing you've ever said to me. Singular, indeed!"

"Besides, it makes you look ridiculous," Ashington said, damping his friend's happiness. He raised an eyebrow in Freddy's direction. "What have you occupied yourself with of late, my Fred?" he asked. "Haven't seen you at the clubs in an age. Taken the veil, have you?"

"Just resting up for the Season. It's barely started, but I'll need my strength to make it through the next few months."

"Ah, yes, the Season," said Ashington gloomily. "I'm not sure I can survive another one, Freddy. All those callow girls, all those scheming mothers! Will it never end?"

"Not until you marry," said Freddy. "Face it, Ash, you're the biggest catch in the puddle. Until someone lands you, the rest will never stop trying. You're too big a fish, dear boy."

Ashington made a face. "Thank you so much, Freddy. I don't believe I've ever before been compared to a mackerel."

"The truth is the truth, dear boy." Freddy slid a look at Ashington. "Speaking of marriage," he said casually, "rumour has it that you and Lady Blandford are on the verge of betrothal."

Ashington choked on his brandy. "What?" he cried. "Dash it all, Freddy, was there ever such a malicious, gossip-ridden Town as London?"

"Don't blame the tattlemongers, Ash," Freddy said. "If you will persist in living in the fair Diantha's pocket..." He shrugged.

"Far from living in her pocket," Ashington snapped, "it just so happens that I have broken with her!" He stopped, then laughed ruefully. "Damn you, Freddy, for goading me into such a piece of gross indiscretion."

"Worry not," said Freddy soothingly. "We aren't in public. And it isn't very likely that I'll go round repeating your words, is it? So you've parted, have you?" He pursed his lips and whistled soundlessly. "I daresay she rang a damnable peal over you; never saw a red-headed chit yet that didn't have the temper of a devil."

Ashington made a face. "She took it rather well, as it happens," he said. "Perhaps a little too well; I fear she may nurture hopes of our reconciliation."

"You probably weren't brutal enough," Freddy said cheerfully. "That's always been your problem with women, Ash; you're too kind."

"Really?" drawled Ashington. "I seem to recall a certain opera dancer—"

"Oh, Freddy, look! My new dresses have arrived. Do you like this one? I think it positively gorgeous." Katherine skipped into the drawing room in a yellow silk ball gown, skirts held daintily up. She stopped dead on the doorstep at the sight of Ashington. "Oh! Oh, excuse me!"

"Don't go, Kate," said Freddy. "Stay and meet my friend Ashington. You'll be seeing quite a lot of him, I daresay. He's in and out of here so often you'd think it was his home." The colour had first drained from Katherine's face, then returned until her cheeks were an alarming shade of red. Freddy turned to Ashington. "Ash, say good day to my cousin, Miss Katherine..." He stopped in confusion. Too late did Freddy realize that Katherine's name would be instantly recognized by Ashington; it would raise all sorts of awkward questions about the girl's antecedents. "Ah—ah..."

Ashington had risen smoothly to his feet when Katherine entered the room. He frowned at Freddy, then crossed the room to take Katherine's hand. "Apparently Freddy has lost what few wits he ever possessed," he said. "I am, as your cousin managed to recall, Lord Ashington. And you are Miss...?"

"Crest!" burst out Freddy. "That's it, Miss Katherine Crest." He took the handkerchief that he had used to polish his glass and mopped his forehead with it. "Uncommon warm in here, ain't it?" he said.

"Not particularly, Fred. No doubt you are overheated by the unaccustomed use of your brain," said Ashington. "I suggest that you sit down and rest yourself." He examined Katherine's costume and smiled. "I agree with you, Miss Crest; your outfit is most fetching. Madame Renée, I believe?'' He had named the foremost dressmaker in London.

''Yes, my lord.'' Katherine spoke in almost a whisper. She could not raise her eyes to Ashington's face; she felt as though she had entered a dream, but whether it was fantasy or nightmare she could not decide.

''I thought so,'' said Ashington. ''One can always discern—''

''I must go,'' Katherine interrupted him. ''Good day, my lord.'' In a swirl of dark hair and yellow silk she was gone.

''So much for genteel conversation,'' said Ashington. He seemed unsure whether to be amused or offended.

''Don't mind Kate,'' said Freddy quickly. ''She's lived a quiet life... isn't really accustomed to gentlemen as yet.''

''Who is she, Freddy?'' asked Ashington curiously. ''I would have sworn that I knew all your relatives, yet I've never heard you mention any Crest family.''

Freddy gave an uneasy laugh. ''Well, I'll wager you don't know nearly as much about me as you might have thought, Ash. For instance, have I ever told you about the time I...'' He trailed to a halt as Ashington turned to stare at him, and mopped his forehead again with the handkerchief.

"What are you up to, Freddy?" asked Ashington suspiciously. "Cut me no gammon, my boy; I'm no green lad, to be taken in by a parcel of nonsense."

Freddy spread his hands and tried to look innocent. "I'm not up to anything," he said. "Just thought I'd invite a country cousin up to stay. The random charitable impulse, don't you know."

Ashington stared at him for another long moment, then shrugged. "Very well, Fred, if you won't tell, you won't tell," he said finally. "I daresay it shall all become clear to me in the fullness of time. Frankly, though, I can't quite picture you in the role of chaperon."

"Oh, I shan't be the one to squire her about," Freddy said hastily. "Aunt Honoria will see to all that."

"Aunt Honoria!" Ashington began to laugh. "Good Lord, Freddy, aren't you afraid that Honoria will lose the poor girl?"

"Or worse yet," chortled Freddy, "can't you just see her inviting some prospective suitor to examine my cousin's teeth?"

When at last their laughter had subsided and Ashington had wiped his streaming eyes, he said, "Fred, you have saved me. I was positively dreading the start of another Season, but with this to look forward to, 'Od's breath, man! I can barely wait for it to begin."

Freddy said, "You might do me a little favour, then, Ash, in return for all this amusement."

Ashington swept his friend an exaggerated bow. "Anything, Fred," he said. "Anything at all."

"Help me keep an eye on Kate, won't you?" Freddy asked earnestly. "Mean to say, hate to see her make a dashed cake of herself with some loose screw because she don't know any better."

"You never fail to amaze me, Frederick Basingstoke," Ashington said. "Are you actually sitting there asking me to help you chaperon Miss Crest?"

"I'm not her chaperon, Ash, I told you that already," Freddy protested. "Just help me... brother her. We'll be like elder brothers to Kate. All right?"

"Very well, Fred," Ashington agreed resignedly.

"Don't look so downcast, Ash," Freddy said happily. "Why, between watching over Kate and eluding the fair Diantha, it's shaping up to be a very exciting Season after all."

HENRI L'ECUSSON BARRED the door and extinguished the last light left burning in the shop. The young man did not immediately go upstairs; he stood for some moments staring blindly out at the moonlit street, running his hand restlessly over a bolt of fabric.

"Henri! Is something amiss? Come upstairs now," Marie called. "Henri?"

"Yes, Maman, I'm coming." Henri turned and climbed the stairs heavily. "I was just locking up."

Marie frowned up at her son, her small arms akimbo. "What is it, my son?" she asked. "What is wrong?"

"Why, nothing, Maman, why do you ask?"

"Nothing? Bah! I am not blind, Henri, or stupid. You have not been content for more than a week now. What is it?"

"I suppose that I'm just missing Kate," her son said, sitting down and leaning his head back against the divan. "It will pass, Maman."

Marie sighed. "Ah, it is hard, is it not? But this is such an opportunity for her! And she will be home soon enough."

Henri sat up straight. "You're joking, of course," he said, then stared at her. "You are joking, aren't you?"

"I don't know what you mean," said Marie.

"Oh, God!" groaned Henri. "Maman, listen to me. Katherine will never come home again, not to live, and very rarely otherwise."

"What are you saying? But of course she will."

"No, Maman, she won't," Henri said. "Why did you arrange all this for her?" he asked.

"So that she might find a husband and restore our family fortunes," Marie answered.

"And what do you think will happen if she does find a husband?" he asked.

"Why..."

"Exactly," he said. "How can she say to her affianced husband, 'By the way, *chérie,* I am not really the French cousin of Monsieur Basingstoke...'"

"They *are* cousins," Marie said defensively. "Not first cousins, it is true, but still related."

"Not the cousin of Basingstoke, but a tailor's sister. You don't mind, do you, *chérie?*" Henri continued inexorably. "What do you imagine a well-situated English lord would have to say to that, Maman?"

"If she waited until after they were married," Marie said, "it would be too late for her husband to object."

"Do we really want to condemn her to that? A lifetime of shame and resentment?" he chided his mother gently. "No, once she is married we must all but disappear from her life. Oh, perhaps she will be able to slip away to see us now and again, but..." He shrugged.

"Oh, no, Henri. I could not bear it!" Marie seemed on the verge of tears, then she blinked her eyes once or twice and shook her head firmly. "It will not be so," she said. "It cannot be. No one could see Katherine and be with her, without loving her, at the last if not at the first. She will win over her husband and he will accept her past and her family. It is not as if we were not *de naissance noble,* after all."

"Can you really have spent all these years among the English and not have learned anything about them?" Henri asked his mother. "They will never accept us, no matter what your birth. We are tradespeo-

ple, no more, no less. That is all that we shall ever be."
He closed his eyes again with a sigh. "For myself, I
have always felt more French than English, though
I've never even set eyes on France."

"You take too gloomy an outlook, my son," said
Marie, her cheerfulness restored. "Have faith in your
sister, Henri. She will overcome these minor difficulties and surprise you, in the end!"

"THAT WAS AN AWFULLY close call, Kate," Freddy
said. "I almost choked."

"I still don't understand why you had to make up
that awful name," Katherine grumbled. " 'Katherine
Crest,' indeed."

"I told you, Kate. Ashington has been to your
brother's shop many times. He would definitely have
recognized the name L'Ecusson. We can't afford to
raise any questions about your background."

"I am not ashamed of my background, nor of my
name," Katherine said hotly.

"Of course you are not," Freddy answered soothingly. "But your mother has gone to a great deal of
trouble to make this come-out possible for you. We
wouldn't want to ruin it before it even begins, would
we?"

"No," acknowledged Katherine. She looked up at
Freddy. "But isn't it possible that he...that they would
accept me anyway?" She lifted her head proudly. "My
birth is as good as anyone's!"

Freddy shook his head. "Ah, Kate, but that is not the way of the world. Even if you could prove your lineage to the satisfaction of the ton, they would still turn away from you and speak dismissingly of 'the odour of the shop.' It is not pretty, is it? But life is what it is and no amount of repining will change it."

A glimmer of amusement lit Katherine's unhappy countenance. "Such profundity, Freddy," she said. "I never would have thought it of you."

Freddy grimaced. "I am not as much a fool as I appear to be, Kate. After all, how could I be? 'Twould surpass reason!" He was surprised by Katherine's burst of laughter. "It is good to see you smile, my dear. You're an uncommon pretty girl, taken all in all." Katherine laughed even harder; Freddy frowned at her, puzzled.

"Oh, Freddy," Katherine gasped finally. "I do like you, however much I might wish that I didn't."

He was pleased. "That's good, Kate. I like you, too!" He frowned again. "There is just one small difficulty..."

"What is that?"

He spread his hands wide. "How in blazes are we going to get Aunt Honoria to learn your new name in time for the ball?"

"What ball?" Katherine asked blankly.

Freddy tugged at his lip. "Lady Rankin's ball, to-morrow night," he said absently.

"Tomorrow night! Why didn't you tell me?" Katherine wailed.

"Didn't Aunt tell you? There's nothing much to be concerned about. It's too early in the Season for any really large entertainment. This will be something fairly intimate, I'm sure."

"How intimate?" Katherine asked suspiciously.

Freddy shrugged. "A hundred or so invited guests, I would imagine," he said.

"A hundred people! Freddy, I'm not ready," Katherine said. "Really, I'm not."

"Nonsense," Freddy said, and patted her hand. "You'll do nicely, my dear, very nicely indeed."

"Oh, but Freddy—"

"Don't worry, Kate." Freddy was on his way out the door as he spoke. "I'm off to find Honoria. You needn't give it another thought. I'll see to everything."

"That," said Katherine aloud to the empty room, "is precisely what I'm worried about!"

CHAPTER FOUR

IT WAS ALMOST nine o'clock, but the polished wood floor of the ballroom held only a handful of guests. Rows of footmen stood motionless along the walls; hundreds of candles made the long room as bright and as warm as day, and intensified the aroma of the banks of flowers piled at either end of the chamber. The orchestra had just begun to play, more for purposes of tuning and readying their instruments than of entertaining those few already present.

These guests were mainly the families of young ladies in their first Season. The damsels had so teased and cajoled their parents that they had, albeit reluctantly, agreed to come rather earlier than was fashionable. This parental want of resolve had been well repaid, however. Several of the earlier arrivals had suffered the ultimate indignity of entering the ballroom before their host and hostess were down to greet them.

Such was no longer the case. Lady Rankin, overwhelming in puce satin, and her milksop husband had positioned themselves by the wide doors that led into the ballroom and were prepared to greet the partygoers who were now beginning to arrive in force.

Edwin Rankin had momentarily managed to escape his parents. He ran a finger under his highly starched neckcloth and grumbled to his friend Ingham, "I wonder how long it will be before we can slip away?" He waved and smiled at his mother, who had fixed him with an icy stare. "Not soon enough," he added gloomily. "My mother will see to that."

"Don't be such a crêpe-hanger," his friend advised him. "Who knows? You may very well enjoy yourself."

"I doubt it," Edwin said. "My mother will see to that, too." He leaned towards Ingham. "Confidentially, Ingham, I think she has it set in her mind that I should marry this year. Can you imagine?"

"Well," said Ingham tactfully, "sooner or later, Edwin..."

"Later," said Edwin. "Much later! I'm too young to get caught in parson's mousetrap. Although," he added, "if I could find a bride like that...!" He dug his elbow into Ingham's side.

The Countess of Blandford walked slowly towards the two young men, enjoying Rankin's open admiration. She was dressed in a low-cut golden silk gown, gathered tight under the bosom and falling in folds to the ground; the fabric clung to her limbs as she moved. A gold ribbon was threaded through her red curls, and diamonds flashed at her neck and wrists.

"I could hardly imagine anything less bridal," Ingham murmured. Edwin Rankin swallowed a laugh as Diantha joined them.

"What's so funny, Ingham?" Diantha asked sharply. Ingham said nothing. Edwin opened his mouth to answer her, but thought better of it after a look from his companion.

"Ah, er, nothing, Di," he said hastily. "Damn, but you're in looks tonight! Won't you save me the supper dance?"

"Don't be absurd, Edwin," Diantha said, her attention still on Ingham. She raked her eyes over him with a slow, derisive look that would have made a lesser man quail. Ingham seemed untroubled by her regard. "You're not looking well, Ingham. I certainly hope that you're not falling prey to your father's malady?"

Ingham paled. His father, it was widely rumoured, had died from an overfondness for drink along with women delicately referred to as 'little barques of frailty.' "No, Diantha, I am not," he said. "If I were, though, I should imagine you would be the first to know."

Once again, Edwin Rankin was obliged to swallow a laugh. Diantha flushed an angry red and stepped closer to Ingham, only to have a restraining hand laid on her arm.

"Good evening, children," said Lord Keswick languidly. "Are you quarrelling? I shouldn't like to miss anything."

"You missed nothing, Kes. Pray excuse me," said Ingham with a tight jaw. He left them and Edwin trailed behind.

"Now I wonder what you've said to make Ingham so angry, my dear?" asked Keswick. "Something particularly noxious, I'd guess. He looked livid."

Diantha waved her hand. "I really don't care what Ingham thinks," she said. "I have more important matters to concern myself with."

"Ah, yes, the assault on Ashington," Keswick said. "I daresay this evening is along the lines of an opening sortie?"

"Oh, Kes, how ridiculous you are."

"Am I, Di?" he said. "And what is this?" One long finger lightly touched the necklace that sparkled at her throat. "His parting gift?"

Diantha tossed her head. "A gift, certainly, but we are far from parted," she said. "Before this evening is over, he will be dancing to my tune again."

One mobile eyebrow soared. "Would you care to lay a small wager on that, my dear?" said Keswick. "Say, five hundred pounds?"

"Done," said Diantha instantly.

"Or better yet," Keswick pressed her, "shall we make the stake your new trinket?" Diantha's hand flew to her throat. Keswick sneered, "Too rare for you?"

Diantha lifted her chin. "Agreed!" she said. "But what if I win, Kes? What will you give me?"

"Why, anything that you desire," he said easily. "If Ashington leaves the ball with you this evening, you may name your own price."

Diantha's eyes glittered. "You're a fool, Keswick," she said, and with a mocking curtsy, moved off into the crowd.

Lord Keswick watched her go with an unreadable expression on his face. Leaning back against the wall, he stood for some time, perfectly at ease, then made his way to the doorway just in time to encounter Lord Ashington.

"Good evening, Ashington," Lord Keswick said. "What a delightful surprise! I had not thought to find you here this evening."

"Keswick." Ashington nodded curtly.

Keswick turned to survey the rapidly growing throng. "Lady Rankin must be in her glory," he remarked. "Her ball bids fair to be a resounding success."

"Indeed," said Ashington, his lack of interest apparent. "If you'll excuse me, Keswick . . ."

Lord Keswick laughed. "Not even the pretence of civility, eh, Ashington? Do you think yourself so far above us all that you need not even observe the barest forms of politeness?"

"Above all? No," Ashington replied, placing the faintest stress on the word *all*.

"Ah," said Keswick. "I see; just above myself." He chuckled. "The insufferable Lord Ashington—so firmly convinced of his own moral superiority that he does not deign to consort with lesser mortals. I find your attitude most puzzling, my lord. After all, what is the difference between us? I amuse myself with women, I freely admit, but do you not do the same? 'Tis a matter only of degree.''

Ashington stared at Keswick. "Degree? I think not, Keswick. The women in my life have all been women of experience; they know the nature of their relationships with me from the very beginning. You, on the other hand, appear to delight in seducing the innocent and the pure."

Keswick shrugged. "One might say that if they were so very pure, they would not allow themselves to be seduced. Women are women, Ashington; they are put on this earth for no other purpose than to please men. I do no more than my part in making use of them. But speaking of women," he continued, "I believe that Diantha is looking for you. Have you thrown her over, my friend? A tedious woman, I agree, but what a magnificent body."

"Have you forgotten, my lord, that no gentleman discusses a lady in public?" Ashington's tone was silky.

"I have not, but it may be that my definition of what constitutes a lady is a trifle more strict than yours." Keswick's voice was no less smooth than Ashington's.

"Be warned, Keswick," Ashington said. "Lady Blandford and I have gone our separate ways, but I will allow no man to slander her, as I would allow no man to slander any lady of my acquaintance. Do I make myself quite clear?" Blue eyes met brown; a long silence fell between the two men.

"I apologize, Ashington," said Keswick finally. "I certainly meant no offence."

"It would be as well," said Ashington, "if you did not speak of Diantha, offensively or otherwise. Remember it, Keswick." Ashington bowed gracefully and was gone.

In a short period of time, the ballroom had been transformed. Now the chamber was full of people, laughing, dancing, gossiping and observing other gossipers. The gowns and jewels of the women made a whirling kaleidoscope of colour; this effect was enhanced, rather than diminished, by the black evening clothes chosen by the vast majority of the gentlemen. The temperature of the chamber had risen to a stifling level and had given a number of young couples the excuse they needed to slip off to the still chilly gardens for 'fresh air.'

Freddy Basingstoke and Katherine had stopped just inside the ballroom doors. Honoria had already left them, to drift off and find such cronies of hers as were present.

"Freddy, I'm frightened," said Katherine breathlessly. "It's all so overwhelming."

"Nothing to be frightened of, Kate," said Freddy. He squeezed the arm tucked into his own and laughed. "After all, you've already made it over the first hurdle...Aunt Honoria remembered your new name!" Katherine giggled. "And," Freddy added, "I daresay you're the prettiest girl here."

Katherine blushed. While Freddy's words were not strictly true, she knew that she looked well in her new yellow silk. Though the shade would not have flattered many of her colouring, it somehow seemed to bring out the highlights in her dark hair, and made her blue eyes sparkle.

"Look, Kate, here is someone you already know," said Freddy. He gently pulled her farther into the room.

"Oh, no, Freddy, don't—"

"Ash!" called Freddy.

Ashington smiled into Katherine's eyes. "Good evening, Miss Crest," he said. "How well you look this evening; a charming frock, if I may say so?"

Katherine's blush deepened. "Thank you, my lord."

He took her hand and kissed it.

"My cousin is feeling a trifle intimidated," Freddy was saying. "This is her first entertainment of any size; pray tell her that there's nothing to be frightened of, won't you, Ash?"

"I'll do better than that," Ashington said. "Miss Crest and I shall perambulate, thereby driving the other gentlemen present mad with envy and curiosity. Shall we, Miss Crest?" Ashington offered her his arm.

"I shouldn't wish to impose, my lord," said Katherine hastily. "And Aunt Honoria may be looking for me."

Freddy and Ashington both laughed. "Kate," said Freddy, "you shall be very lucky indeed if we see

Honoria again all evening. The call of the whist table is irresistible to her.''

Katherine opened and closed her mouth, then said in a small voice, "Very well, then. Thank you, my lord.''

Ashington and Katherine moved off into the crowd. Katherine was very aware of the strength of Ashington's arm, and for his part, Ashington could feel the hand on his arm trembling. For a moment, he covered it with his own. "There really is nothing to be afraid of, Miss Crest," he said. "They are only people.''

"To you, my lord," said Katherine. "You have grown up among them. But for a stranger..." Her voice trailed off.

"Where did you grow up, Miss Crest?" he asked, as they wound their way among the groups of guests along the edge of the dance floor.

"In France," said Katherine quickly. "I've only just come to England.''

"Really?" said Ashington. "I must congratulate you on your English, then. You have no trace of an accent that I can discern.''

"I...er...had an English governess.''

"Ah, that would explain it," said Ashington. He bowed gracefully to a passing couple, then continued. "Have you any other family besides Freddy and Aunt Honoria?''

"Aunt?" Katherine said. "Are you, too, kinsman to Freddy?''

Ashington shook his head. "No, but by reason of being acquainted with both of them since childhood, I call Honoria aunt, and think of her that way, too."

"I see," said Katherine.

"But you never answered me; have you any other family?"

"Yes, my mother and an elder brother," Katherine said, then added, "I miss them both quite dreadfully!"

"Did they not accompany you to England?"

Katherine shook her head, and Ashington felt a sudden burst of sympathy for this girl, so young and so obviously overwhelmed by her introduction to the ton. He patted the small hand that lay on his arm and said, "Well, we shall just have to see to it that you are too busy enjoying yourself to pine for them, then." He smiled down at her. "What do you say, Miss Crest? Will you lend yourself to our plan and allow Freddy and me to amuse you while you are in Town?"

Katherine, feeling as though her throat would burst if she tried to speak, could only nod her head and wonder dizzily if all ladies in their first Season felt so wonderfully, gloriously happy!

LORD KESWICK MADE A sweeping bow before Lady Rankin. "My dear Lady Rankin," he murmured. "How very ravishing you look this evening." In point of fact, Lady Rankin had been most unwise to choose puce satin for her gown; the dark colour made her look sallow and pale, and the satin increased one's impression of her girth, which was already formidable.

"Do you think so, my lord?" Lady Rankin simpered. "My modiste actually had the temerity to imply that I had made a poor choice. Well! You may be sure that I put the ungrateful creature in her place."

"Very wise, my lady," Keswick said. "It would never do to allow the lower orders to take advantage of one's good nature."

"Exactly," said Lady Rankin with satisfaction.

"Your ball is . . . what can I say? A triumph," Keswick continued. "Never have I experienced so glittering an entertainment so early in the Season. You are to be commended."

Lady Rankin looked even more gratified. "Thank you, my lord," she said. "Coming from one so sophisticated as yourself, such praise is doubly flattering. It *is* going well, isn't it?" She looked round the ballroom, and her brow furrowed in irritation. "Will you look at that? 'Tis too, too vexing."

"My lady?"

"Will you look at that son of mine? Standing by the potted palms, talking with that odious Freddy Basingstoke. Why does he waste his time there? He should be looking for a rich . . . That is to say, he should be cultivating the acquaintance of some suitable young lady."

Keswick saw his opportunity. "Perhaps he is," he suggested. "I noticed that Basingstoke arrived with a young lady on his arm this evening. Who is she, do you know?''

Lady Rankin shrugged. "Oh, some young cousin of his, from somewhere or other; I can't recall at the moment. Why? Is the chit…" She paused, then added delicately, "suitable?"

"I don't know," Keswick responded. "But I have noticed that Lord Ashington seems to have an interest there. He has been most attentive to the child this evening, most attentive indeed."

"And isn't that just like him?" Lady Rankin said, exasperated. "I mean to say, if the girl is … suitable, 'twould be just like Ashington to make himself the focus of her attention, when it doesn't matter a whit whether he marries a rich girl or a poor one. I do not call that the action of a well-bred guest, I take leave to tell you. After all, does it not stand to reason that in all politeness, one should allow one's host, or one's host's son, first shot at a fortune? 'Tis only good manners!''

"I agree with you wholeheartedly," Keswick said, smothering a laugh. "So the girl is … suitable?"

"Oh, as to that, I have no notion," Lady Rankin said peevishly. "Honoria Basingstoke did no more than introduce me to the chit before flying off to the whist tables. I daresay Freddy would know, though; why don't you ask him?"

Keswick spread his hands wide. "I am not that interested, my lady, I assure you. 'Twas merely idle curiosity that made me ask."

Lady Rankin tapped a finger thoughtfully against her teeth. "I wonder, now," she mused. "Freddy hasn't two shillings to rub together, everyone knows that, but Honoria is quite well off, quite well off indeed. Do you think the child might be an heiress?"

"As I said, my lady, I don't know who or what she is. By the way, what is her name?"

Lady Rankin's brow wrinkled in thought. "Caste, I think, or something like it . . . Crest! That's it: Katherine Crest."

"Would you be good enough to introduce me to her?" Keswick asked.

Lady Rankin peered up into Keswick's face. "What, have you an interest there, Keswick?" she said in surprise. "I wouldn't have thought her your type at all."

"And you would be right," Keswick replied easily. He tucked Lady Rankin's arm into his own and prepared to lead her across the room to where Katherine was dancing, with Lord Rankin himself. "Let us just say," he said, almost under his breath, "that I am interested to see what Ashington finds so attractive in her."

ASHINGTON FLIPPED the butt of his cheroot off into the garden and stepped back into the ballroom. Lady Rankin must be ecstatic, he thought, for the premier ball of the Season had turned out to be a smashing success. The ballroom was packed; through the doors thrown open at the end of the room he could see that the tables set up for cards were likewise beset. He watched the dancers swirl and turn before him and wondered if it were late enough for him to leave. He had found, over the past two or three Seasons, that the social scene had begun to pall for him. He had spent too many years, he supposed, doing the same things with the same people. Perhaps he should go down to Woldtoft; the very emptiness of his country seat would be a refreshing change from the crowds and constant activities of London. He should stay in London, he knew; to begin with, he had made a promise to Freddy to help him squire Miss Crest through the Season. It was also past time for Ashington to be thinking of marriage, and he would never find a bride immured in the wilds of the country. But somehow he no longer cared to look; it was stubborn and wrong-headed of him, perhaps, but if he could not marry for love, he preferred never to marry at all. Unfortunately, he had begun to think that he would never find a woman whom he could love for a lifetime. He had been infatuated and aroused, but never deeply, permanently touched by any lady of his acquaintance. If it had not happened by now... Suddenly, Ashington's train of thought was broken and his brows snapped together in a frown. He strode across the room.

"Excuse me, but I believe that Miss Crest promised me this dance," he said.

Lord Keswick tucked Katherine's arm more firmly into the crook of his own and replied smoothly, "Ah, but you are too late, Ashington. To the victor the spoils.''

"I think not," Ashington said flatly.

Katherine looked back and forth between Ashington and her companion, bewildered.

"Don't be tiresome, my lord," Keswick said softly. "'Twould be a pity to make a scene." The air between the two men fairly crackled.

"You're right, of course," answered Ashington as softly. "Though I would not have thought to see you display such nicety of behaviour, at this late date."

Keswick's eyes narrowed. "Be careful, my dear Ashington," he said. "Be very careful."

"I...I think Lord Ashington is right about the dance," Katherine said, frightened by a sudden sense of danger. "Will you forgive me, my lord?"

Keswick stared at Ashington, blue eyes icy, for what seemed to Katherine an eternity before finally turning back to her. "Most assuredly, exquisite one," he said, with the smile that had melted many a maiden's heart. "In truth, I can scarce blame Ashington for his importunity. To win such a prize, who would not persist?" He pressed a kiss onto her hand, one that left Katherine breathless. "I do not say farewell, my dear, but only *au revoir*. I shall expect you to save me the next dance."

Ashington and Katherine watched Lord Keswick walk away, then Ashington took Katherine by the hand and swept her out onto the floor. She felt dizzy, as if only the strength of Ashington's embrace kept her from sinking to her knees in the middle of the crowd.

"You would do well, Miss Crest, to learn to discourage the advances of such as Lord Keswick," Ashington said.

"What?" Katherine's head recoiled as though she had been slapped.

"It does a lady's reputation no good to be branded as fast," he continued coldly. "Flirt with a roué and that is exactly what will be said of you."

Katherine could feel the hot blood flooding into her cheeks. "Flirt? Encourage? I don't know what you're talking about!"

"Pray do not feign stupidity," Ashington said. "You know very well—"

"I know very well, my lord, that whatever I do, 'tis no concern of yours," Katherine interrupted him. "And I was not flirting."

Ashington sighed. "What an oaf I am," he said. "I am forgetting, of course, how quietly you have been raised." He smiled down at her. "Am I forgiven?"

"I . . . Yes, I suppose so," Katherine said, and immediately regretted the grudging sound of the words. They danced on for a moment or two, then Katherine asked hesitantly, "My lord?"

"Yes?" Ashington's tone was cool. He had apologized manfully, he thought, and if she chose to pout, it was her own affair.

"I do forgive you, but what is wrong with Lord Keswick? Lady Rankin introduced him to me. I should have thought, if Keswick were not quite the thing...."

"The lady is sometimes less than wise, Miss Crest."

"But he seemed so agreeable," Katherine persisted. "Quite unexceptionable, as Freddy would say."

"In London, Miss Crest, one must be exceedingly outré to be noteworthy," Ashington said dryly. "You may not always trust in appearances."

"I simply don't understand," Katherine said.

"No, you don't," said Ashington, good humour restored, "and that is what one particularly likes about you. You are an innocent, Miss Crest."

"But—"

"Pray don't trouble yourself." Ashington squeezed the hand that lay so trustingly in his own. "I'll have a word with Freddy about it." He lifted his eyes from the crown of Katherine's shining black hair and found himself facing Keswick across the floor. Keswick was watching Ashington and Katherine, his expression unreadable.

The music stopped; all around them couples began to move off the floor. Ashington deliberately turned away, but he could still feel Keswick's eyes boring into his back. *Damn the fellow!* he thought, and said to Katherine, "Since we foolishly wasted so much of this dance quarrelling, let's have another, shall we?"

Katherine could only agree, and she and Ashington twirled off into the crowd.

LORD KESWICK WATCHED Ashington sweep Katherine away for a second dance and turned from the dance floor. He saw the Countess of Blandford standing nearby and walked over to join her. The redheaded woman stood glowering at the dancers, one foot tapping impatiently.

"Ah, Diantha," he said. "I see you've noticed Ashington's little companion."

"Who is she?" Diantha demanded without preamble.

"Freddy Basingstoke's cousin," Keswick said. "His country cousin, to be precise."

"Freddy's cousin? I should have known." Diantha smirked. "She has that homely Basingstoke face, though her colouring is quite different."

"Do you think so?" Keswick said, openly enjoying Diantha's discomfiture. "Ashington does not appear to agree with you."

Diantha's face darkened as she watched Ashington smile down at Katherine. "Oh, well, you know Ash," she managed finally. "Ever the gentleman! 'Tis just like him to take an interest in one lacking . . . shall we say, certain charms?"

"I have never known Ashington to be quite so altruistic, myself," Keswick said. "Of course, I bow to your greater knowledge of him."

"Yes, I daresay that dancing with such a one makes Ashington feel charitable," said Diantha. "Men are so childish about such things."

"Are we? I had not noticed it."

"Not you," Diantha said with a brittle laugh. "I daresay you have never had a charitable impulse in your life."

"Quite right," Keswick said briskly. "Speaking of which, it begins to appear that I shall win this evening's wager quite handily. I should like to collect my winnings as soon as possible. Shall we say tomorrow morning? I'll meet you in Hyde Park at nine o'clock."

"You have not yet won," Diantha blustered. "The night isn't over. I still have time!"

"Perhaps," Keswick replied, "but since my lord Ashington has already committed the social solecism of dancing with Miss Crest twice running, I daresay he won't hesitate to sit in her pocket all the rest of the evening, too."

"He never did!" Diantha gasped.

"But yes, I promise you that he did, indeed," Keswick said. "Look about you at all the tabbies gossiping and casting baleful glances at Ashington and Miss Crest; can you doubt it?"

In truth, Lord Ashington had caused a certain amount of talk by standing up with Miss Crest twice. Diantha could clearly see one old dowager shaking her head in disapproval; several other older women were whispering furiously, and Lady Rankin appeared to be giving her cowed-looking son an angry, if low-voiced raking down, with frequent pointed glances directed at Ashington and his companion.

"Oh, well," Diantha said airily, her colour high, "I'm sure Ashington was simply trying to be kind."

"That may be true," allowed Keswick. "But ask yourself, Diantha; why should Ashington be so very kind to her, yet so very cold to you? *Au revoir*, my pet!"

Keswick might have saved his words. Diantha had barely noticed his departure. In the midst of the light and colour of Lady Rankin's ball, Diantha stood alone, her attention focussed solely on Ashington and on the dark-haired child who might, Diantha thought sickly, prove to be her greatest threat.

CHAPTER FIVE

"I MUST HAVE BEEN MAD to let you talk me into this,"
Freddy groaned, blinking his eyes against the harsh
morning light. "Absolutely mad." He tooled his curricle flawlessly around a tight corner and out into the
street.

"Not mad, Freddy—gallant, as always," Katherine said in great good humour. She raised her para-
sol, unconsciously setting it at a becoming angle, and
smiled up at him. "And I am most grateful, I promise you."

Freddy was not immune to such feminine flattery.
"Oh, well, it's nothing," he said modestly. "Though
really, Kate, I can't think why you'd want to go to the
Park at this hour. The place will be dashed well deserted."

Katherine smiled. Freddy looked at her, more suspiciously this time. He asked, "What are you up to,
my girl?"

Katherine opened her eyes wide. "Why, Freddy,
whatever do you mean?" She could not quite contain
a trill of laughter.

"Kate!"

"Well, if you must know, I'm going to meet my brother," she said.

"Your brother... Kate, what are you thinking of? You can't be seen with Henri. You can't afford to start people wondering." Freddy was appalled.

"Oh, Freddy, pray do calm yourself," she said. "You just finished telling me that no one would be abroad in the Park this early in the day. What could be safer?"

"Not seeing him at all, that's what," said Freddy. "Lord, Kate, it's too risky by half."

"I don't care," Katherine said. "I miss Henri, and I'm going to see him. If not here—" she gestured as they pulled into the Park "—then at the shop."

"At the shop...!"

"Exactly," Kate remarked dryly. "Oh, Freddy, I miss my family," she said. "Is that so hard to understand? I never wanted to go through with Maman's plan in the first place, you'll recall. I did so because she wished it. And I haven't sulked or been uncooperative, have I?"

"No," Freddy admitted reluctantly. "You've been game as a pullet, Kate, that I must allow."

"I don't belong here," Katherine said. "I belong back at the shop, with Maman and Henri. Can you understand? This is not my world."

"Now, Kate, you must admit, you have been enjoying yourself," Freddy said. "Why, think of Lady Rankin's ball; you had a wonderful time, you can't deny it." Katherine blushed. She could not argue with

Freddy's words, for she had left Lady Rankin's ball feeling as though she could leap and caper for joy. "Besides," he added earnestly, "this *is* your world, or should be. Dash it all, you're as well born as I am. Better, maybe."

"Would the rest of the ton agree with you, Freddy?" Katherine asked sadly. "Would Lady Rankin have invited me to her ball, had she known who I really was and where I really came from?" Freddy did not answer. "I thought not," she said.

"Oh, Kate," Freddy said.

"Never look so sad, cousin," said Katherine, in a lightning change of mood. "I said I'd go through with this masquerade and I shall. Just don't object too much when I need to see my family. Agreed?"

Freddy shrugged. "Agreed," he said.

"Look, Freddy, there he is. Put me down, put me down!"

"Oh, no," her companion said grimly. "If you must visit him, you'll just have to put up with me while you do it, my girl. I can always say that I was speaking to Henri, if anyone should see us. Though they'd think me wits-to-let," he muttered as he pulled over, "for standing in the Park conversing with my tailor, of all people!"

DIANTHA, COUNTESS of Blanford, scowled at the couple walking away from her through the trees, Freddy Basingstoke ambling along a step or two behind them. *That girl!* she thought. The chit might have been set down here just to annoy her. She swiped viciously at a shrub with her riding crop and kicked the long skirt of her green velvet habit out behind her. All the previous evening Diantha had brooded about the girl with the heavy black hair. However bravely Diantha might have spoken to Keswick, she knew it was not like Ashington to show such distinction to any young woman, Freddy Basingstoke's cousin or no. Ashington's attentions to the child had been singular; in addition to dancing with her twice, he had made a point of stopping to speak to her and Freddy before he left the ball. Diantha was deeply troubled by Ashington's interest in Miss Crest. The thought that Katherine might replace her as Ashington's mistress would not have troubled Diantha half so much as the certain knowledge that if Ashington were interested in the girl, it was as a bride, not a mistress.

Diantha watched the retreating trio closely, her brow puckered. She knew the girl's companion, she realized suddenly. She couldn't remember from where, but she had definitely seen him before. If only she could remember...

"I give you good morrow, dear Diantha," a voice purred in her ear. "A nature watch, lovely one?"

Diantha jumped. "Keswick!" she snapped. "Must you sneak about so?"

"Sneak?" Lord Keswick yawned delicately, one slender hand raised to cover his mouth. "I fail to see how you can accuse me of sneaking, when meeting me is the very reason you're here."

Diantha turned away from him; he peered over her shoulder. "Ah, La Crest!" he said. "Of a sudden I understand your bile, Di. She put your nose properly out of joint last night, didn't she?"

"I don't know what you're talking about," Diantha muttered.

"Come, come, my sweet. Ashington could barely drag his eyes away from the child all evening." Keswick yawned again. "It was all the talk, as I told you."

"People are stupid," Diantha growled. "Ash was merely being courteous, that's all." She took another turn about the small clearing. "You can't possibly think him interested in such a horsey, polelike creature?"

"She's hardly so repulsive as all that," Keswick said. "Rather a fetching little thing, in fact."

"Little?" shrilled Diantha. "Lord, Kes, she's almost as tall as you are."

"'Tis strange," said Keswick musingly. "I have the distinct feeling that I know this girl from somewhere, but I can't seem to recall..." He pulled at his lip thoughtfully with his long, slender fingers. "Perhaps I should make it my business to learn a little more about the mysterious Miss Crest."

"Mysterious? What's mysterious about her?" Diantha snorted. "She's just some little nobody from nowhere."

"Never tell me that you believe this nonsense of Basingstoke's about a long-lost cousin, my dear?" Keswick asked. "I had thought you too much the downy one for that! Are you not the least bit curious about the lady who looks likely to steal my lord Ashington away from you?''

"I told you, Kes, he's not—"

"Ashington most certainly is interested," Keswick interrupted her. "He all but knocked me down to get at Miss Crest last evening, and made it his business to see that I had no further opportunity to speak with her. He was most unmannerly. It may be that I shall have to teach friend Ashington a lesson."

"You?" Diantha said maliciously. "You must be all about in your head, Keswick. If there were a lesson to be taught, Ash would be the one teaching it."

"That's as may be," said Keswick imperturbably. "But I believe that we did not come here this morning to discuss Ashington's newest interest. My winnings, please, Diantha." He held out a hand.

Diantha stepped closer to him. "Surely you're not going to take my necklace, Kes?" she said. "You can't be so cruel."

"Ah, but I can, my dear."

"It isn't fair," Diantha cried, stamping her foot. "I never had a chance to get near him. That whey-faced, missish little—"

"Temper, temper," Keswick said mockingly. "Banish Miss Crest from your mind, Di. Had you been the only woman in the room, Ashington would not have cared. He's through with you."

"No," said Diantha. "I can't believe it. I won't believe it! He loves me, I tell you. He loves me!"

Lord Keswick shrugged. "He has a strange way of showing it," he remarked. "But all of this is neither here nor there. My necklace, please."

"And what if I won't give it to you?" Diantha said defiantly. "What then, Kes?"

Keswick looked down at her. "Why, I could just take it," he said. Diantha shrank away from him; he laughed. "But I wouldn't need to, would I?" His blue eyes were steely. "Pay or play—that is the philosophy the beau monde lives by. Your birth has entitled you to a great deal of tolerance, by way of your liaisons, Diantha, but it would not excuse a refusal to pay in a matter of honour."

"Such niceties apply only to gentlemen," Diantha said, an edge of desperation in her voice. "A lady may ignore—"

"Not a lady," Keswick interrupted her, "who relies so heavily upon the forbearance of gentlemen. Need I say more, Di?"

"I despise you," she hissed.

"So you've told me, many times," Keswick said. "Frankly, sweet, you're fast becoming a bore on the subject. Once again, though, it doesn't signify. Just give me my winnings, that I may go home and to bed. It's been a long night."

Diantha pulled the necklace out and hurled it at Keswick. It glittered in the sun, and Keswick admired it for a moment before shoving it into a pocket. "Thank you, my dear," he said. He bowed. "I'll be sure to use this to good purpose."

"May you burn in hell, Keswick!"

"I may," he said, moving off through the trees. "But if I do, 'tis certain that I'll meet you there."

ASHINGTON STOPPED before a mirror in the foyer to check his already impeccable neckcloth and to rearrange slightly the perfect yellow roses he carried. He smiled to himself; bringing a lady a bouquet of flowers after having danced with her might be a dated custom, but it was one that he thought might please Katherine Crest. He entered the drawing room, but stopped on the threshold, frowning; the room appeared to be empty. Then he heard a low humming from behind the davenport and crossed the room to find Lady Honoria Basingstoke sitting cross-legged before the fire, toasting crumpets on a long fork.

"Aunt Honoria," he said, his eyes alight with laughter. "You look most comfortable."

"Good day, Ashington," said Honoria. She smiled vaguely up at her guest. "Would you care to join me?"

"But of course," he said. With no regard for the state of his clothes, he hunkered down to join her. "Crumpets!" he said. "Lord, I haven't toasted a crumpet since my nursery days."

"The more fool you," said Honoria. "There is nothing so good, I think, as a crumpet one toasts oneself." She slid her browned crumpet off the fork and solemnly proffered the instrument to Ashington. "Looking for Kate?" she asked, eyeing the roses.

"Why, yes," said Ashington. He neatly slid a crumpet onto the browning fork and held it over the fire. "Where is she? Still abed?"

"No, she's gone out with Freddy," said Honoria. "To the Park." She took a bite of her crumpet and chewed it thoroughly before continuing, "I'm just as glad, really. I wanted to talk to you."

"Oh?"

Honoria took another bite. "Do you plan to marry Kate?" she asked.

"What?" Ashington was so startled that he dropped the fork, crumpet and all, into the fire.

"What a pity," said Honoria. "Let me ring and have Croaker bring you another."

"Forget the damn . . . that is to say, it is of no importance," said Ashington. "What do you mean, do I plan to marry Miss Crest? Of course I don't!"

"I thought not," said Honoria calmly. "It seemed as well to be sure, all the same. One never can tell about these things."

"But what made you ask such an absurd question?" Ashington said. "I barely know the child."

"It's not as though it weren't past time that you wed," Honoria went on, intent on her own thoughts. "You are the last of your name; 'tis your duty to marry and have children. And Kate would, I am sure, make you as good a wife as any young lady could. Are you quite sure . . . ?"

"Yes," snapped Ashington, "I am! And if you don't tell me what started you on this extraordinary course of conversation, I'll..."

"Yes?" said Honoria pleasantly.

"Die of curiosity," he finished lamely.

Honoria laughed aloud and patted Ashington on the knee. "You are a good lad," she said, "however thoughtless you may be at times."

"Thoughtless?" Ashington repeated, then said, "Ah! I begin to perceive..."

"Exactly," said Honoria. "You made Katherine the subject of a great deal of unpleasant speculation by your attentions to her at Lady Rankin's ball. You danced with her twice and hovered over her like the most jealous of lovers all evening. What were you thinking of, Ashington?"

He shrugged uncomfortably. "Just doing the pretty," he said. "Trying to make her comfortable, and seeing to it that she enjoyed herself. Freddy did ask me to help, you know."

"Balderdash!" said Honoria bluntly. "You didn't make such a cake of yourself only to help Freddy. What was it? If you aren't attracted to the girl..." She fixed Ashington with a piercing stare.

"It was Keswick," he confessed. "I was only trying to protect Miss Crest. Keswick was watching her the way a hungry dog watches a meal."

"So?" said Honoria. "She's a very pretty girl. Why shouldn't he watch her?"

"It isn't fit for an innocent young thing like Miss Crest to have anything to do with such a one as Keswick," Ashington said; even as he spoke, he realized how stiff and stodgy he sounded. "I take leave to tell you, Aunt Honoria, that if you had been playing chaperon instead of whist, I shouldn't have been obliged to!"

"What nonsense," said Honoria. "Lord Keswick is extremely eligible; there's no reason on Earth that Kate shouldn't get to know him. Why, he might make her a very good husband."

"How can you say such a thing?" Ashington exclaimed. "Think of his reputation! The man's no better than a roué."

"He wouldn't be the first gentleman to reform for the sake of true love," Honoria replied. "The tales of reformed rakes are so common as to be . . . well, commonplace."

"True love?" Ashington said in disgust. "Keswick doesn't know the meaning of the word love."

"None the less, Ashington, you had no right to behave as you did," said Honoria sternly. "Whatever may or may not transpire between Keswick and Katherine is her affair and, to a lesser extent, mine. Not yours, Ashington; be very clear about that, if you please. The question is, how do we stem the flood of gossip that your behaviour started?"

Ashington looked sheepish. "As to that," he admitted, "I've already seen to the matter."

Honoria looked intrigued. "Do tell," she said. "I know you wield a great deal of power among the ton, but to be able to stop the busybodies? I am impressed."

"I went to Lady Jersey..." Ashington began.

It was Honoria's turn to exclaim. "Sally Jersey?" she said. "A woman who lives to gossip? They don't call her 'Silence' out of kind impulses, you know."

"I know, I know," Ashington said. "But she and I have always been quite friendly. She does have a soft heart beneath all her brittle sophistication, you know."

"Oh, I see," said Honoria sarcastically. "Just from loving kindness, she agreed to help squelch the story?" Honoria did not for a moment dispute the fact that Lady Jersey could stop it, if she so chose; as she was a leader of Society and a Patroness of Almack's, any member of the ton would be loath to court Lady Jersey's displeasure by repeating a story of which that lady disapproved.

"No" said Ashington. "I simply reminded Sally of the days when she first came to London, before she was wed, and of how lonely and unhappy she was. Then I pointed out to her that my only objective at Lady Rankin's was to make Miss Crest feel a little more at home. Sally agreed to do what she could to stop the gossip."

"Well!" said Honoria, sitting back on her heels. "I must say, Ashington, you've handled the matter quite well. Not that you shouldn't have, mind, since it was your fault to begin with, but you've done quite well, nonetheless. Thank you.''

"Don't thank me," said Ashington. "As you said, it was all my fault." He looked at Honoria soberly. "But if you'll take my advice, Aunt Honoria, you'll watch Miss Crest and keep her away from Keswick. He'll do her no good, of that you may be sure."

"You may safely leave it to me to see to Katherine's interests," said Honoria briskly. "Of one thing you may be sure, though; no man will trifle with my Katherine unless he first puts a wedding ring on her finger!"

CHAPTER SIX

"AH, LADY BASINGSTOKE! Good day to you." Lord Keswick shut the door silently behind him and crossed the room to bow over his hostess's hand.

"Keswick?" Honoria looked surprised. "Didn't that fool of a butler of mine tell you that Freddy's not at home? He's taken Katherine to see the Tower of London. Can't think why the girl wanted to visit such a musty, depressing sort of place, but there! She's half French, you know."

"No, I didn't know," Keswick said. "And your butler did tell me that Freddy was not at home but, as I came to see you, 'twas not of any great interest to me."

Honoria's eyes focussed on Keswick. "Now, why would you want to see me?" she asked. "Hoping I'll supply you with a juicy on-dit to repeat in company?"

Keswick blinked. "I assure you, my lady, I—"

"No matter," she said and waved him into a seat. "I daresay your purpose will become clear, in time."

Keswick blinked again. "I must admit, Lady Basingstoke, I have never seen you quite so...sharp."

"Oh, I'm not half so daft as the gossips would have me," Honoria said, pushing her hair back off her forehead. The resulting disarray to her coiffure did little to substantiate her claim. "I daresay you'd like a brandy?" She did not wait for Keswick to answer her, but filled two glasses. Keswick watched in fascination as she tossed back the spirits, then belched noisily. "There is nothing," she declared, "that so takes the chill off a day as a glass of brandy." As it was a mild April morning, Keswick could only assume that old bones felt the cold to an exaggerated degree.

"So," he began again. "Are you enjoying the Season, my lady?"

"Tolerably well," she replied. "'Twas a blow when old Lady Trine decided to stay in Bath for the Season, I will admit, but I've managed to bear up under the disappointment."

"Is Lady Trine a particular friend of yours?" Keswick asked.

"Lord, no! I detest the woman, have since we were both girls. Since my husband died, though, I've had so little to occupy me that I've quite devoted myself to plaguing the old harridan." She sighed gustily. "Such things are sent to try us, are they not?"

"Quite," said Keswick. He decided to try another tack. "You must be enjoying Miss Crest's visit."

"Miss Crest?" Honoria repeated blankly. "Oh, you mean Kate! Yes, it has almost made up for no Lady Trine, having the girl about. She quite enlivens this old place." Honoria slanted an amused glance at her visitor. "Have you an interest there?"

Keswick shrugged. "I should not go so far as to say an interest," he said. "Rather, a curiosity."

Five hundred years of breeding showed suddenly in Honoria's cold expression and the drawling tones in which she said, "Pray indulge your curiosity with someone else, Keswick, not with my cousin."

Keswick held up a hand. "No, no, Lady Basingstoke, you misunderstand me," he said, chagrined at his own lack of subtlety. "Say, rather, that I am intrigued by the young lady, and wish to know a little more about her before I pursue the connection further."

Honoria's expression did not noticeably thaw. "Are you suggesting, my lord, that a kinswoman of mine might be unacceptable to you?"

Lord Keswick smiled charmingly. "I can see," he said, "that I've made an awful hash of this. All I wanted, dear Lady Basingstoke, was to learn a little bit more about Miss Crest. I had an ulterior motive, I freely admit... I hoped to use the information to endear myself to the lady. Have I sunk myself beneath your reproach?"

Honoria relented. "Why didn't you say so?" she demanded. "You would not be much of a man if you didn't try to cut out your competition."

"Exactly so. And my visit has already proved profitable; I was not aware that Miss Crest was half

French." He paused. "Though I do not quite see the connection with your family?"

"Through my Aunt Lucinda," Honoria supplied. "She was Kate's great-aunt." She eyed Keswick again. "You might do very nicely for Kate," she said musingly. "I've always held that older men are better for young girls than boys their own age. A steadying influence, don't you know."

"Such considerations are a trifle premature, Honoria," Keswick said, trying to keep his distaste from showing. "I've only just met Miss Crest."

"You're too old by half to procrastinate," Honoria said sharply. "I don't understand you young gentlemen today. In my time, a man was leg-shackled before he had the chance to learn anything of the world. Much better that way, in my opinion; there's plenty of time to gain experience after marriage. Now, my Kate would make you an excellent wife—she's pretty and well-bred, and there's nothing missish or milk-and-water about her."

"Alas, those are not the only considerations," Keswick said. "You understand... The demands on one's resources..." He shrugged delicately.

"You wish to know if she's well-fixed?"

"I should not have put it quite that way, but yes, I did wonder," Keswick said.

"By God, Keswick, but you do remind me of your papa," Honoria said; not without a certain indulgence. "Just like you, he was...forge ahead and damn the consequences. He came to a bad end, of course. That heedlessness is a dangerous trait.''

"You won't think me too rude if I say that my father is not the subject at hand?'' Keswick's tone was silky.

"Don't pucker up at me," Honoria said cheerfully. "That infamous temper of yours don't frighten me in the least." She smiled. "Ah, well, I've ever had a weakness for a rogue," she said.

"How very gratifying," he murmured.

"As to Kate's fortune, it would be most improper in me to discuss it," she said, "but suffice it to say that she is not without resources." Honoria was not certain that this was strictly true, but honesty seemed a small price to pay to secure a suitable match for Kate.

"I see," said Keswick uncertainly.

"Apparently you do not," Honoria said. She silently threw caution to the winds. "To be quite crude, my lord, Katherine is more than able to supply any gentleman with not only the necessities of life, but also its luxuries." She waited a moment, then added, "And let me ask you this, Keswick. Do you think Ashington would have shown the interest he has, to a girl who was not hosed and shod?" Honoria watched Keswick's eyes narrow and then widen a little. She almost chuckled in satisfaction. She had done the best she could for the girl, she reflected. After all, it might be true. Mightn't it?

FREDDY WAS still grumbling. "I don't know why you drag me to all these confounded places, Kate," he said. "The Tower, Lord Elgin's marbles, St. Paul's... Is there a musty site in London we haven't seen?"

"Several, as a matter of fact," Katherine said briskly, consulting a small guidebook. "Perhaps we can go again tomorrow."

"Oh, no," said Freddy, shaking his head. "I'm da... dashed if I shall. As it is, I don't know how I'll ever live it down. I was seen at the Tower, I'll have you know."

"No, Freddy...this is awful!" Kate's eyes twinkled. "How will you ever bear the shame of it all?"

"Yes, yes, you may well laugh," said Freddy gloomily as he helped her out of the carriage. "Your friends won't think you've run mad. Why, I daresay they'll be talking about me in the clubs for weeks. My only hope is that they won't believe Sanderson, but he's such a dull dog that they probably will."

Katherine went into the house on a trill of laughter. "Poor Freddy," she said as they entered the drawing-room. "I'm sure your consequence will survive the incident."

Honoria rose to her feet. "Kate," she said. "Perfect timing, my dear. Lord Keswick was just asking after you."

Keswick did not betray his irritation as he greeted Katherine. "Good day, fair one," he said. "I understand you've been seeing the sights of London. Did you enjoy your jaunt?"

"Very much, my lord," said Katherine in a subdued voice. Try as she might, she could not help but recall Ashington's warnings about her visitor.

Freddy, too, did not seem overly fond of their guest. "'Lo, Keswick" he said coolly. "What brings you here?"

Keswick did not seem to think the question rude. "Why, your beautiful cousin, of course," he answered. "I was hoping that I might offer her my services as an escort. Surely you have not exhausted the historical bounty of London in just one day?"

Katherine was touched by his consideration. "Why, thank you, my lord. Freddy was just saying—"

"I was just saying that there's nothing I'd rather do than show Kate about London," Freddy broke in. "Wouldn't dream of missing it, no, not for any consideration."

"Freddy!" protested Katherine. "You did not. You said—"

"I insist." It was Keswick's turn to interrupt. "I must claim for myself the pleasure of introducing Miss Crest to the British Museum. Tomorrow morning, perhaps?" He slanted an enigmatic look at Freddy. "You've no objections, have you, Freddy?"

Freddy opened his mouth but Katherine forestalled him. "Thank you, my lord, I should love to," she said, with a glare at Freddy.

"Lady Basingstoke!" Diantha, Countess of Blandford, blew into the drawing room in a swirl of velvet and lace. "I knew you wouldn't mind if I saw myself in, such old friends as we are. How are you, dear lady?" Honoria looked blank. "It is I—Lady Blandford," the young woman said. "You are such a tease!" She turned to the rest of the company. "Good day, Freddy, Kes." She fixed a sharp eye on Katherine. "And you must be Miss Crest," she said. She held out a hand.

Katherine smiled uncertainly. "Good day, my lady."

"Oh, no, call me Diantha," the newcomer said. She squeezed herself down next to Katherine. "And I shall call you Kate. That is your name, is it not? I have the feeling we shall be great friends, you and I."

Keswick swallowed a laugh. "That," he murmured, "would be wondrous indeed!" Katherine looked at him, puzzled, but Diantha ignored the comment.

"Tell me all about yourself, Kate," she invited. "You have the ton all in a buzz, you know. We do not often entertain beautiful strangers from...France, is it not?"

"Yes," said Freddy.

"No," said Katherine.

"That is to say," Freddy said quickly, "Kate was raised in France but has been in England for quite some time, at school."

Lord Ashington paused on the threshold of the drawing-room, his brow puckered. English schools? he thought. But had Miss Crest not told him...?

Diantha caught sight of him. "Ash," she said warmly, leaping to her feet. "What a naughty boy you are! If you had told me that you were to call on Kate, we might have come together." She squeezed his arm.

Ashington disentangled his limb. "Good morning, Diantha," he said. He crossed to his hostess. "I give you good day, Aunt Honoria," he said. He bent down to murmur in her ear, "What? No crumpets?"

"Don't pitch me your gammon, boy," Honoria said sharply and rose to her feet. "I've no time to waste with you young here-and-thereians." She took the sting out of her words by pinching his cheek affectionately. "I'm off to see to the arrangements for Kate's ball. I'll leave you to deal with our visitors, Ash. Lord knows, I haven't the slightest notion what they're all doing here." She paused for a moment, then added truthfully, "Except for Keswick, and he's a little too like his papa to be trusted, don't you think?"

Ashington swallowed a laugh. "Indeed I do, Aunt Honoria," he said as that lady left the room.

"Your aunt is become somewhat strange, Freddy," Diantha said. "I daresay you shall have to do something about her one of these days."

"I beg your pardon?" Freddy said frigidly.

"Oh, Diantha is just put off by Lady Basingstoke's honesty," said Keswick. "'Tis not a quality with which our Diantha is overly familiar, is it, love?"

"Kes..." hissed Diantha.

"'Tis a lovely day, is it not?" Katherine put in desperately.

"It is indeed," said Ashington. He settled himself down beside her. The girl blushed and tried to ignore the strength of Ashington's leg, so close to her own. "Are you enjoying your stay in Town, Kate?"

"Kate?" tittered Diantha unpleasantly. "I had not known that you and Miss Crest were so close, Ash."

"But then, there is a great deal that you do not know about me, Diantha," said Ashington, pleasantly enough. The woman flushed.

"So we are agreed then?" said Keswick to Katherine. "Tomorrow morning?"

Katherine was aware of Ashington's eyes on her. She lifted her head proudly and said defiantly, "We are, my lord. I shall be ready."

Diantha was surreptitiously observing Katherine's profile. Distantly, she heard Keswick say, "Well, I shall be off, then. To my tailor's to be exact. I've a yen to order a coat from this new shop you've discovered, Ashington, this L'Ecusson."

As he spoke, the blood suffused Katherine's face; she dropped her gaze to her clenched hands.

Suddenly, Diantha knew where she had seen the young man that Katherine had been with in the Park. She smiled vindictively, barely able to conceal her exultation.

"Pray don't let us detain you, Keswick," said Ashington.

Freddy shook his head at the rude remark, but Keswick made no reply. He bowed ironically and moved to the end of the room. As he passed Ashington, something bright dropped from his pocket to the floor. Without thinking, Ashington bent to pick it up, then stopped.

"Where did you get this?" Ashington asked.

Diantha sucked in her breath. "Keswick! What are you doing?" She cursed her own lack of foresight. She should have known that Keswick would use the necklace to humiliate Ashington. "Ash," she began desperately. "I—"

"It was a gift," Keswick said. "From a friend. A lady friend." He smiled triumphantly, but his triumph was short-lived.

Ashington met Keswick's eyes for a moment, then he dropped the bauble into Keswick's outstretched hand. "Here you are," he said lightly, and turned his attention back to Katherine.

"Ashington," Diantha burst out. "Please..."

"Thank you, my lord," said Keswick. He spoke to Katherine. "Until tomorrow, fair one."

Lord Ashington did not watch Keswick leave. He smiled at Katherine and said, "I was sorry to have missed you yesterday."

"I was, too," Katherine said. "I must thank you for the roses, my lord. They are so very beautiful!" She raised her eyes to Ashington's face. "I've never been given flowers before," she confessed shyly. "Oh, a posy or two from my brother on my birthday, perhaps. But never any half so lovely, and never from..." She stopped in confusion.

"A gentleman?" Ashington supplied helpfully.

Katherine nodded. "It made me feel so very grown up!" she added ingenuously.

Ashington chuckled. He was touched and absurdly pleased by the notion that he had been the first gentleman to give Katherine a nosegay. "I may have been the first, my dear, but I won't be the last, I promise you. You'll take the Town by storm, Kate."

Katherine blushed, but was spared the necessity of answering by Croaker's arrival with the tea tray. After Katherine and Lord Ashington had helped themselves, Croaker carried the tray across the room to Freddy and Diantha.

Diantha was watching Ashington and Katherine closely. She watched the colour rise in Katherine's cheeks and decided that it was time she intervened. She waved Croaker away and made as if to rise, but Freddy, watching her as closely as she was watching Ashington, spoke.

"I say, Diantha," he said, "what do you like for the Derby?" He could not have chosen a subject more likely to distract Diantha's mind; she was an avid gambler, just as happy betting on the progress of two raindrops down a pane of glass as a horse race.

"I don't know," she said, half her attention still on Ashington and Katherine. "What do you think?"

Freddy waited until Croaker had departed, then leaned closer to Diantha. "I think well of this filly Roundaboutation," he said. "Her owner, Lord Devlin, assures me that she's in top form and can easily beat anything on four legs."

"Really?" Diantha's attention was well and fully caught. "But what about the Two Thousand Guineas? As I recall, she only came in third there."

"Devlin swears it was the jockey; claims the lad pulled back on the home stretch. I'm inclined to believe him. I went down to Newmarket last week and watched the horse in training, and I must say, she does look smashing."

Honoria entered the room and crossed over to join Freddy and Diantha. Freddy appealed to his aunt. "I say, Aunt, what do you think of Roundaboutation?"

"Not good," Honoria said. "A waste of everybody's time."

"But, Aunt! It did very well in it's last outing," Freddy said earnestly. "Left everything else in the dust."

"Roundaboutation may benefit you in the short term," said Honoria, "but in the long run, I predict naught but damage."

"Do you mean that you think the course too long for it?" Diantha asked.

Honoria favoured Diantha with a long and sceptical look, then said firmly, "Plainspeaking—that's what I hold with."

"Plainspeaking," mused Diantha. "I'm not sure I'm familiar with that..."

Honoria gave a crack of rude laughter. "Now that is the most honest thing you've said today!"

Diantha sniffed and turned her attention to Freddy. "As I was saying," she said, "I'm not familiar with Plainspeaking—is it a filly or a colt?"

"Must be a colt," Freddy said. "With a name like that.... How did it do in the St. Leger?"

Honoria looked back and forth from Freddy to Diantha. "And they call *me* mad!" she said.

Across the room, Ashington was speaking. "So, where were you and Freddy off to, yesterday?"

"We went to the Park," Katherine replied.

Ashington nodded. "Hyde Park is very beautiful at this time of the year. Perhaps you might like to go for a drive there with me tomorrow?"

Katherine flushed. "I'm sorry, but I have another engagement." Then she added defiantly, "with Lord Keswick."

"I see," said Ashington quietly. "Perhaps some other time."

"Yes," agreed Katherine. A small silence fell between them. Katherine felt obliged to say, "I know that you do not quite like my friendship with Lord Keswick, my lord, but I must tell you, he has been everything that is most kind to me."

"That may well be," Ashington said. "He has the most polished of manners, of that I am fully aware."

"But?" Katherine prompted.

"But manners may be deceiving," Ashington said. He took Katherine's hand in his own. "I know it must seem to you," he continued, "as though I am a stuffy old fool, and an odiously interfering one at that."

"Oh, no, not at all," Katherine assured him.

"'Tis just that I have a care for your welfare. I should hate to see you become put in a position that you might find...uncomfortable," Ashington said carefully.

Katherine looked up at him, her eyes glowing. "Really?" she said. "You really...worry about me?"

"Er...yes," he said. "I do worry, and with good reason, when it comes to Keswick. Won't you reconsider your decision to see him tomorrow?" Ashington met her gaze squarely. He found himself seized by the fanciful notion that time had stopped, that everything in the world had paused for this moment. The blue of her eyes was deep and inviting; Ashington wondered if any man had ever kissed her, and found himself powerfully disturbed by the notion.

"I—I..." Katherine stammered. She felt a curious difficulty in breathing, as though there were a weight planted firmly in the middle of her chest.

Ashington could sense her indecision. "I have nothing but your good at heart," he said, ruthlessly squelching all thoughts of Katherine as a woman. "Think of me as a brother, my dear, an elder brother filled with concern for you."

Katherine's head rocked back on her shoulders as though she had been struck. *A brother?* she thought. He thought of himself as her brother? And she had been ready to cancel her outing with Keswick for him! "I appreciate your concern, my lord," she said, amazed at the cool, controlled sound of her own voice.

"But I must tell you, I would not allow my own brother to tell me with whom I may or may not associate. I thank you for your care for me, but I am quite capable of seeing to my own interests."

Ashington made one more try. "Please, Kate," he began.

"The subject is closed, my lord," she said.

"Very well," said Ashington stiffly. "You are, of course, free to do as you think best. I only hope," he added grimly, "that you will have no cause to regret this freedom."

CHAPTER SEVEN

"IT WAS MOST KIND in you, my lord, to have brought me here," said Katherine to Lord Keswick the next morning. "I fear that it cannot have been very much to your liking." The deserted gallery in which they stood bore ample testimony to the fact that the Museum was not as popular a haunt of the ton as was the Pantheon Bazaar or Bond Street. Katherine had enjoyed her viewing of the collected art works, so much so that she was ashamed to recall that it had been only her feeling of anger towards Ashington which had finally decided her to come.

"Not at all, Miss Crest," replied Lord Keswick, "though I do admit 'tis not a place graced often by my presence." He grimaced expressively and stopped before a painting by Sir Joshua Reynolds. "I am far too frivolous a creature for edification. Besides," he continued, "here I am all too likely to encounter a gentleman of this ilk." He indicated the subject of the painting. "A courtier of Charles II, I believe. A sad rake, not unlike his sovereign." Keswick turned blue eyes on Katherine. "He is far too sharp a reminder of my own failings, I fear."

"Surely...surely you are not so very bad, my lord?" Katherine asked.

Keswick shrugged gracefully. "That would depend," he said, "on whom you asked. Were it Ashington, now... I freely admit that I have not lived the life of a monk, these many years I've been in London. But neither have I lived the life of a reprobate." He shrugged again. "It is my own fault that Ashington maligns me. I do not amuse myself with the circumspection that my lord employs."

"Oh" was all that Katherine could think of to say.

"Indeed," he said, "The Lady Blandford and Ashington have employed a level of discretion quite remarkable in two such...imperious...personalities. But that is neither here nor there."

Katherine did not speak. She was stunned by the notion that Ashington and the Countess of Blandford were lovers; how could she have been so blind? How could she not have noticed? Now she realized the significance of the countess's long looks at Ashington, and the proprietary air which that lady adopted whenever she spoke of him. *What a fool I have been,* she thought, *not to have realized!*

Though he perceived his companion's discomfiture, Keswick hid his satisfaction. "Well, my dear? Have you seen quite all that you wish to see?"

Katherine nodded mutely.

"Perhaps I should take you home, then," he said. "Freddie has become positively gothic in his concern for you, Miss Crest. I have never seen the dear boy display so much ferocity."

Katherine composed herself enough to say, "He is good to have such a care for me, is he not? We have not, after all, known each other..." She stopped, appalled at what she had been about to say. *Stop this foolishness,* she told herself fiercely. *What Lady Blandford and Ashington are to each other is nothing to you!*

Keswick waited a moment, then prompted her, "Yes? You have not known each other...?"

"From...from the cradle," Katherine faltered.

One of his lordship's brows swooped upwards. "Indeed?"

Keswick's curricle drew up just as they reached the steps outside; Katherine wondered fleetingly how the groom had managed it. Keswick helped Katherine to settle herself in the vehicle and took up the reins beside her. "From Freddy's protective attitude towards you, one would think that he had known you from infancy," he remarked as they pulled into the busy street. "He reminds me of nothing so much as a jealous young dog guarding a bone." He sighed lugubriously. "No doubt because I myself am so far removed from youthful ardour."

Katherine smiled, only too happy to change the subject. "Oh, I fancy that you will not sit by the fire sucking your gums yet a while," she said. "Lord Keswick is known everywhere as an out-and-outer, is he not? The tailors fight to dress you; they all say that you make the clothes. You and . . . someone else," she finished lamely.

Keswick took his eyes off the road for a moment and looked at Katherine. But what an extraordinary thing to say! he thought. How would this child know what tradesmen thought or said?

Katherine seemed to realize her mistake, for she added, "Or so it is said." Keswick made no response; they travelled the rest of the way back to the Basingstoke residence in silence.

"Well, Miss Crest?" said Keswick as he saw her to the door. "May I call on you again, though Ashington dislikes it?" He watched her face closely as he spoke.

Katherine flushed. "I cannot think why you would imagine that Ashington's opinion is of the least importance to me," she answered.

"Freddy, then," Keswick pressed her. "He does not approve."

"Freddy may be my cousin, but he is not my keeper," Katherine retorted sharply. "As long as Aunt Honoria does not object . . ."

"Excellent," said Keswick. He bowed over her hand. "I shall strive to stay on the most excellent of terms with the blessed Honoria, then. *Au revoir, ma belle.*" He bowed and watched Katherine walk into the house. *So!* he thought. *You are already half in love with Ashington, aren't you? And my lord Ashington is not indifferent to you, either.* Keswick wondered if he should ruin the little Crest girl, just to upset Ashington. It might be amusing, he thought, and jumped into his curricle.

The tall man set the horses in motion with a sharp gesture that made the parchment in his pocket crackle. Keswick frowned; the communication from his solicitor weighed heavily on his mind. The old fool! However bad his financial situation might be, it was the grossest impertinence for the lawyer to write to him in such a vein. Keswick irritably shook the reins. "Desperate straits," indeed! There was nothing else for it, then, but to find a rich wife. But whom? Someone young and malleable, with no close relatives to interfere with his treatment of her, Keswick mused; a young lady of looks and, of course, immense fortune. Keswick did not sell himself short. Despite his reputation and the fact that he was over forty, he was still a prime catch on The Marriage Mart. Keswick's hands tightened on the reins. *Why not Miss Crest?* he thought suddenly. She would be perfect! She met every one of his requirements, with the added fillip of being the object of Ashington's desire.

Lord Arthur Keswick smiled, and startled his horses by snapping his fingers. "Done!" he said aloud with a laugh. Miss Katherine Crest would be his route to financial comfort and the instrument of his revenge on Ashington, at one and the same time.

KATHERINE WALKED SLOWLY up the stairs towards the drawing-room, lost in thought. Keswick's casual mention of the liaison between Ashington and Diantha, Countess of Blandford, should not have shocked her, she knew. In spite of her quiet upbringing, Katherine was not wholly ignorant of the ways of the world. She had heard Maman and Henri discuss the on-dits of the day often enough—which gentleman was a rake, which a gambler, how all Society was talking about the latest opera dancer to be in Lord So-and-So's protection. It was much less common, though, to hear such gossip about a lady. It was not totally unheard of, of course; there was Lady Harley, Countess of Oxford, whose children were so numerously fathered that they were known as the Harleian Miscellany. But generally speaking, the ladies of the ton guarded their virtue zealously. Katherine wondered what could possibly have induced Diantha to become Ashington's mistress. Was she so in love with him that she had thrown caution, and her morals, to the wind? In that case, why had the two not married? Katherine was sure that Lady Blandford must want to marry Ashington. Could it be that Ashington was so dead set against marriage that he would not wed even if he were in love? Or was his lordship so proud of his name that he would not give it to any woman with the slightest smirch on her reputation?

However much Diantha's actions might trouble Katherine, though, it was Ashington who tore at her heart. Why, Katherine asked herself, was she so appalled by the knowledge that Ashington was no different than any other gentleman? Gentlemen had mistresses, she knew, particularly young, unmarried gentlemen. *Because,* a part of her answered, *because you thought him better than the rest. The more fool you!* Her eyes sparkled with anger as she castigated herself. Ashington, Keswick, even no doubt, Freddy Basingstoke—they were all the same, she thought. And how despicably hypocritical of Ashington to fill her ears with veiled, ominous warnings about Keswick, a man who was no better or worse than Ashington himself. She would tell Ashington so, she decided hotly, at the first opportunity.

In the drawing room, Ashington turned away from the window, struggling to hold his anger in check. So she had driven out with Keswick, despite his warnings, had she? He had come to call on Katherine with every intention of apologizing for his odiously interfering behaviour; it was her business, he had intended to tell her, to decide with whom she would associate. But seeing Katherine step out of Keswick's curricle had made him forget all that. It seemed incomprehensible to him that the chit should so ignore his warnings. Despite her refusal to discuss her friendship with Keswick with him, Ashington had been sure that her native good sense would lead her to see that Keswick was an unfit companion, and so cancel to-day's outing. And what of Freddy? Why would any gentleman with any sense at all allow his innocent young cousin to be on terms with such a hardened roué as Keswick? He had answered his own question, he thought grimly. No one with any sense would, which left Freddy squarely out of the running.

The drawing-room door opened and Katherine stopped on the threshold. The colour in her cheeks, already high, became even higher. She straightened her shoulders and stepped into the room.

"You went driving with him?" Ashington demanded. "After all my warnings?"

Katherine bowed her head ironically. "Good day to you, too, my lord," she said, stripping off her gloves and tossing them onto a table. "I am very well, thank you. And you?"

Ashington flushed. "Quite well," he said curtly.

"To answer your question, yes, I did go out with Lord Keswick," she said. "We went to the Museum."

Ashington snorted loudly. "He is doing his best to turn you up sweet, isn't he?"

"As I told you yesterday," said Katherine through clenched teeth, "his lordship has been everything that is most kind to me."

"Meaning that I have not?" Ashington shot back. "Because I have more of a care for your reputation and happiness than either you or your dim-witted cousin?"

"As I also told you yesterday," Katherine said, "my reputation and happiness are not your concern. Lord Keswick—"

"Lord Keswick," Ashington broke in brutally, "is after one thing and one thing only. A rich wife!"

"Hah!" said Katherine triumphantly. "That proves how very wrong you are. I have no fortune! Or at least," she added honestly, "nothing that Keswick would call a fortune."

"You may be sure that Lord Keswick is unaware of that fact," Ashington said. "Else he would not waste his time with you."

Katherine gasped in outrage. "You are too, too flattering, my lord! Tell me, then . . . if I am so totally unworthy of a gentleman's attention, why do you trouble yourself with me?"

Ashington opened his mouth to speak, then closed it again. Of a sudden, her question seemed a good one. Why did he have such a drive to protect Katherine, such a feeling of responsibility for a girl he had not known a bare two weeks ago? He had promised Freddy to help keep an eye on Katherine, it was true, but that did not explain his intense feelings of anger when she had ignored his advice. "I don't know," he said finally. "I imagine it's because I like you, very much."

"Oh," said Katherine weakly.

Ashington crossed the room to Katherine and took both her hands in his. "Forgive me," he said. "Though I feel most strongly that Keswick is not a fit companion for you, I should not have spoken to you so sharply."

Katherine could not look up at him. She felt that if she did, he would know how fast her heart was beating and how her knees were hard-pressed to support her.

Ashington took her chin between his fingers and gently lifted her face. "Do you forgive me?" he breathed.

The drawing room door flew open. "Kate!" said Freddy, storming into the room. "Where have you been? I want to talk to you."

Ashington did not lift his gaze from Katherine's clear blue eyes, but he did release her chin. "Ah, Freddy," he said. "Just the man I wanted to see. A word with you, old boy?"

"Er, certainly, Ash," Freddy said, looking back and forth between Ashington and Katherine in some confusion.

"Will you drive with me tomorrow, Kate?" Ashington asked softly. His eyes twinkling, he said, "I don't promise you anything as exciting as the Museum, but I daresay we shall contrive."

Katherine, not trusting her voice, could only nod. Ashington bowed and turned to Freddy.

"Come along, Fred," he said, a dangerous glint in his eye. "We have matters to discuss, you and I."

DIANTHA LOOKED UP and down the dimly lit alley before slipping through the gate. It was dusk, and she wished to enter the yard of the tailor shop before it became any darker. She was almost invisible in the gathering twilight; she had worn a voluminous black cloak to aid in her spying, her red curls forced under a black hood.

Once through the gate, she quickly surveyed the long, enclosed yard which ran behind the row of shops, and chose a spot under one of the long windows that opened out of the tailor shop. Cautiously she raised her head and peered in. There he was!

Diantha had been truly shocked when she had realized, that day at the Basingstoke's, who it was she had seen Katherine meeting in the Park. Despite her own somewhat licentious style of life, she had never, nor never would, she told herself, stoop to cavorting with a tradesman. The Fates had smiled on her, she thought, for whatever interest Ashington might have in that Crest chit would never survive the revelation that the girl was involved with a tailor, of all people.

That was why Diantha had decided to come to L'Ecusson and reconnoitre. Had she just gone to Ashington and told him of Katherine's perfidy, he would never have believed her. The notion that a wellborn girl would so lower herself was simply too fantastic to be believed. So Diantha had come, on her own, to see what else she could learn. Once she had proof, she would see to it that Ashington never looked at Katherine Crest again, she promised herself. If gratitude did not drive him back into her arms, Diantha thought that injured pride would. After all, it would not be very soothing to a gentleman's pride to be cut out by a nobody of a tradesman.

She raised her head again and peeped into the shop. Henri was just locking up and calling something over his shoulder to someone she could not see. She could not hear what he was saying, but she was alarmed that he was now making for the back door of the shop, hard by where Diantha was crouched. She looked about wildly. There was only one place to hide: a small shed that abutted the fence enclosing the yard.

Just in time did Diantha gain the shadows of the shed. She heard the back door open and heavy footsteps approaching her. "Come out!" a low voice called. "You must come out and leave here, right now!"

Diantha's heart was beating so heavily she could hardly hear. She shrank into the corner of the shed, behind a pile of boxes, and held her breath.

"Come out, I say," Henri said in a hoarse whisper. "Come out at once."

"Henri?" called a woman's voice. "What is detaining you, my son?"

"Nothing, Maman," Henri called back. "Go along to bed, now, dearest. You'll never be rid of that headache if you don't. I shall be in presently."

"Very well," the woman's voice said. *"Bonne nuit, mon coeur."*

"Bonne nuit, Maman." Henri pulled open the door of the shed and stepped in. "Where are you?" he asked menacingly.

Diantha shrank deeper into the pile of boxes. Henri heaved an irritated sigh and moved about the shed until he found her. "What are you doing here again?" he asked.

"Don't hurt me!" Diantha squeaked.

"Hurt you? I should like to wring your neck," Henri said. Diantha cowered away from him and he heaved another sigh. "How could you be so foolish?" he asked, towering over her. "Coming here all alone—anything might have happened to you!"

Diantha was regretting her previous cowardice. She stood, drew herself up and said, "But that is none of your concern, sir. If you will be so kind as to step aside?"

Henri had lifted his head and was listening. "Shh!" he said urgently and slapped a hand over Diantha's mouth.

Heavy footsteps approached the shed. A voice called, "I'll jest see ter the shed, afore I go. Wouldn't want them oranges stole, now, would we?" There was a fumbling sound at the door of the shed, then, with heart sinking, Diantha heard a lock snap shut. The footsteps receded, and Diantha bit her captor.

Henri released her and Diantha screamed. "It won't do you a bit of good," he said gloomily. "No one will hear you now. All the shops are closed."

"You may think to have your way with me, sir," Diantha said wildly, "but you shall not, I promise you! I will fight you, tooth and nail."

"That's very nice," Henri said bitterly. "I try to protect your reputation, and these are the thanks I get!"

"My reputation?" said Diantha. "I don't understand."

"Monsieur Paddington is our neighbour," Henri explained. "He is a greengrocer. He caters to all the better households. He would have recognized you, my lady." Diantha's head snapped up. "Did you think that I would not know you?" Henri asked.

"I fooled you, the day I came to your shop..." Diantha faltered to a stop.

"Dressed as a boy?" Henri finished. "No, I merely decided to go along with the joke. I shouldn't have, if I'd ever thought that you would be foolish enough to come back." He stopped. "Why *did* you come back?"

"I...that is to say..." Diantha thought quickly. "I came to talk to you," she said boldly. "I have a business proposition to make to you."

"Another frock coat, madame?" Henri was amused despite himself.

"No," said Diantha. "A letter."

"Pardon?"

"A letter, stating that you are, er, friendly—that is to say, more than friendly—with Miss Katherine Crest." She heard Henri's sharply indrawn breath. "Did you think no one knew?" she asked triumphantly. "You were wrong, monsieur. I know, and soon everyone will."

"I think not," Henri said, after a moment.

"Ah, but they will," responded Diantha. "Even if you don't oblige me with a letter of confession, I shall still find a way to prove it. So why not make it easier for all of us and cooperate? I should be happy to make it worth your while."

Henri's voice sounded sad when he spoke again. "I perceive that you are, indeed, as bad as the gossips would have you," he said. "The gentlemen, they come into the shop and talk, as I fit them; about this one and that, about who is in fashion and out. They tell me that my Lord Ashington has thrown over the Countess of Blandford and that she is wild to get him back. They tell me that she will do anything to get what she wants. I see they are correct."

Diantha was stung by his words. "Do you think to turn me from my purpose by insulting me?" she asked. "It won't work."

"There is no need to insult you for that reason," he said. He turned away from her, so that she could see his profile against the moonlight streaming through the cracks in the door. "You will forget all about telling anyone that Miss Crest knows me," he went on.

"Why should I do that?" she asked.

"Because if you don't, I shall whisper in the ears of my gentlemen the too-amusing story of Diantha, Countess of Blandford, dressed as a boy and roaming the streets of London," he said.

"They would never believe you," she said scornfully.

"Would they not?" he asked. "When the tale reaches Monsieur Rankin, as it will, think you that he will not corroborate my story? Frankly, I am surprised that he has kept silent for this long."

Diantha opened her mouth, then shut it again. Edwin Rankin would delight, she realized, in exposing her. So, too, would Ingham, after the way she had insulted him at Lady Rankin's ball. "It might cause me a little embarrassment," she blustered, "but no more than that. Ashington already knows all about it."

"Ah, but if I also go to Lord Ashington and tell him how you tried to blackmail me, I think he will be angry," Henri said. "Very angry indeed."

Diantha knew this to be true. "Who *is* this girl?" she cried. "Why should you all be so loyal to her?" Henri did not answer her. She looked at the black hair curling on his brow and the deep blue of his eyes and suddenly knew. "You're not her lover," she said accusingly. "That was why I looked at her and remembered you. You are her brother!"

"That, too, is information that you will share with no one," Henri said calmly. He shrugged out of his coat. "I suggest," he added, "that you take this and try to get some sleep. In the morning, when Paddington comes and unlocks the shed, I will slip out first and make up some story about how I was locked in. While I draw him off, you should have time enough to make your escape. *Bonne nuit, madame la comtesse.*" He turned away. Diantha was left to make herself as comfortable as she could leaning against the crates of oranges and to reflect, in the darkness, that it would be a very long night.

CHAPTER EIGHT

LORD ASHINGTON WHISTLED happily as he stood before the mirror arranging the snowy white folds of his neckcloth. His valet, anxiously waiting with an armful of freshly starched cravats, could not help but feel that it ill behooved a peer of the realm to be so cheerful so early in the day. The man frowned dolorously and harrumphed when his master grinned at him in the mirror.

Ashington ripped off the neckcloth with no apparent impairment of mood. "I'll try again, I think," he said, and held out a hand for a fresh cloth. His valet complied. Ashington achieved a creditable result before many more moments had passed, and his servant helped him shrug into his frock coat.

"Tell Higgins that I shall be needing my greys and the phaeton as soon as I've had my breakfast," Ashington said as he left the room. "I'll be taking a lady driving, so tell him to be ready to come with me. I may want him to hold the horses if we decide to stop for a stroll."

Downstairs, Ashington sat down with his coffee and news sheet, but his peace was to be disturbed.

"My lord, there is a Person to see you," his butler announced.

"A Person?" Ashington repeated, amused. "What sort of person?"

"A young woman, my lord," the butler said, as forbiddingly as he dared. "She states that her name is Dorcas and that she must see you immediately."

"Dorcas?" Ashington frowned. "I don't think I... Oh!"

"She says," the butler said, fixing his gaze on a point somewhere above Ashington's head, "that the matter is urgent."

Ashington's frown deepened. "I'll see her."

"Just as you wish, my lord." The butler stood back and held the breakfast room door open.

As Ashington passed the old family retainer, he winked at the man. "You needn't look a thundercloud at me, Stubbs," he said. "She isn't my light o' love, I promise you."

"I would never demean myself by thinking so, my lord," said the butler, but he looked very much less disapproving.

"Oh! My Lord Ashington!" The woman leapt to her feet as Ashington entered the room where Stubbs had left her waiting. "Thank you for seeing me, my lord."

"I can't imagine," said Ashington, "why you should wish to see me." He regarded the maid coldly, then said, "If your mistress has sent you—"

"No, my lord, she hasn't. That's just it, you see."
Diantha's maid wrung her hands and looked as if she
were about to weep. "Lady Blandford didn't come
home last night!"

Ashington's spine stiffened. "That," he said, "is no
possible concern of mine."

"I didn't know where else to turn," Dorcas wailed.

"Perhaps," said Ashington bitingly, "to my lady's
newest . . . companion."

"My lord!" said the maid reproachfully. "That
isn't fair; her ladyship hasn't any companion, right at
the moment. Why, she isn't properly over you yet."

Ashington took a deep breath, angry at Dorcas for
coming to him, but also angry at himself for allowing
his irritation to goad him into such an intemperate and
ungentlemanly remark. "That is neither here nor
there," he said. "Lady Blandford's comings and go-
ings are of no concern, nor, may I say, interest, to
me."

"You don't understand," the woman cried. "She
was engaged to go to Lady Haricot's ball last night."
Ashington looked supremely unconcerned. Dorcas
went on, "She told me she wouldn't miss it for anything, as she expected that Lord and Lady Haricot
would have one of their famous quarrels, which she
says they always do when they entertain. And I had
her green silk all laid out for her, and that beautiful
fan that she got from Lord—" She paused in confusion, then went on, "But she never came home!"

Ashington's mouth twitched, but he said only, "So?"

"Something must have happened to her," the woman said. "Something awful, I fear, especially since..." The maid stopped. She looked up into Ashington's face and suddenly seemed to sag. "I don't know what to do," she whispered. "She is in trouble, I'm sure of it."

Ashington took pity on the servant. Though he was infuriated by the thought of being dragged back into Diantha's life, he could not turn his back on the maid, so obviously and sincerely concerned by her mistress's absence. "Why don't you sit down," he said more kindly, "and tell me why you are so sure that something awful must have happened to her. You needn't be afraid. I won't eat you, you know."

"Oh, my lord, I told her not to do it," the maid burst out. "I told her that no good would come of sneaking out alone, at night, like some kind of hoyden. I told her that she'd be sorry if she did, and sooner than she thought. But she wouldn't listen! She just laughed and told me to mind my own affairs or she'd turn me off."

"She was alone?" Ashington said.

"She was," said Dorcas. "That's what has me in such a pucker, you see."

Ashington felt the first stirrings of real alarm. "Did she take her carriage?"

The maid shook her head. "A hackney cab," she said gloomily.

"Where did she go?"

"I don't know," Dorcas wailed. "I don't know!"

Ashington stood up. "You did right to come to me, Dorcas," he said. "Don't worry yourself any further about this. I shall find your mistress and see her safely restored to you." *But not,* he thought as he shouted for his hat and cane, *not before I say a few choice words to her myself!*

"WHAT? STILL HERE?" Freddy Basingstoke ambled into the drawing room. "I thought you'd be long gone by now."

Katherine managed, with some difficulty, to keep her tone light. "So did I," she said.

"Mean to say, it ain't at all the thing to keep a lady waiting," Freddy commented. "Must be some kind of Lothario."

Despite herself, Katherine laughed. "A literary reference, Freddy? I had not thought you so erudite."

"Erudite? Me?" Freddy blinked. "I wish my tutor might have heard you—he used to tell me that he had read of hearts of oak, but never before encountered a head of oak!" Katherine did not respond. "I'm sorry your swain, whoever he is, has disappointed you," he added gently.

Katherine tossed her head. "I'm not disappointed," she snapped. "In fact, I'm relieved to be spared a tedious and pointless encounter." So saying, she stripped off her gloves and tossed them on a table. She set her bonnet carefully down beside them.

"No need to try to bam me, cos," Freddy said. "I heard you singing while you were dressing this morning. And telling your maid to set out your newest bonnet, what's more. A lady don't wear her best bonnet for nothing."

Katherine ground her teeth. "You're quite mistaken, Freddy."

"All right," Freddy said equably. "Whatever you say." He eyed his cousin for a moment. "With whom were you engaged to go out this morning?"

"Why do you ask?" Katherine responded.

"It wasn't Keswick, was it?"

All Katherine's anger at Ashington for not appearing that morning seemed to boil over. "And what if it was?" she asked. "I should like to know what you have to say about it, Freddy Basingstoke?"

Freddy blinked again, but did not quail. "Well, actually, I have a great deal to say about it," he said. "He ain't the kind of person that you should know, Kate. 'Pon my word, he's not!"

"Really?" she asked with a sniff. "And whose opinion is that, Freddy? Yours, or Ashington's?"

"Both," Freddy said frankly. "Lord, did Ashington ring a peal over me! Asked me in that cursed cold way of his what kind of cousin I was, letting you run about with a roué like Keswick. I didn't know how to answer him."

"I'll tell you how you should have answered him," Katherine said. "By damning him for his impudence!"

Freddy looked shocked. "Here, now, Kate," he began.

She clenched her fists. "Oh, the gall of that man! How dare he interfere in my life, or call you to task for what is patently none of his business? I could throttle him."

"You're making a great deal out of nothing, Kate," Freddy said. "Mean to say, Ashington's only concerned for your reputation. He's trying to protect you, as he would his own sister."

"Sister?" Katherine cried. "What is all this talk of sisters and brothers? I am no sister to him, nor have I any wish to be."

"Be that as it may," Freddy said, sticking valiantly to his point, "you shouldn't be so angry at him for trying to give you the hint about how to go on. He means it kindly."

"I beg leave to tell you, Freddy, that I should not tolerate such meddling from my *own* brother, much less a stranger," Kate said tightly.

Freddy frowned. "Speaking of your brother..." He stopped.

Katherine's anger was immediately replaced by concern. "What about him? Is something wrong?"

"Not precisely," Freddy said.

"What, then?"

Freddy leaned forward in his seat. "I've been hearing rumours," he said slowly. "Rumours about a French solicitor, asking around about some gentleman named L'Ecusson. It's got me puzzled, Kate. Worried, too.''

Katherine appeared blank. "But why would a French solicitor be looking for Henri?''

"I don't know," Freddy said. He gazed warily at Katherine. "He ain't in some kind of trouble, is he?" he asked. "Did he get into a coil in France and come to ground in England?"

"Of course not," Katherine said. "He's never even been to France. And how could he be hiding in England, when his name is on the sign above the shop for anyone to see?''

Freddy looked relieved. "That's true," he acknowledged. "I can't think why this solicitor person hasn't found him already, now that you mention it.''

"If he's seeking a gentleman, it probably hasn't occurred to him to look in a shop," Katherine said. "No gentleman would soil his hands with trade, would he?" She laughed bitterly. "It seems that snobbery and pride are universal, doesn't it? Though my brother is probably one of the easiest men in London to locate, because of his shop, this Frenchman cannot find him. And why? Because it never occurs to him that any gentleman would work for a living. Better to starve, eh, Freddy?''

"No need to take such a tone with me, Kate," Freddy said. "I know you both for what you are— quality, through and through.''

Katherine blinked back sudden tears. "Thank you, Freddy," she said softly.

"Still and all, you'll have to be extra careful while this Frenchman is nosing about," Freddy warned her. "It wouldn't do for anyone to learn who you really are. Imagine if Ashington found out!" Freddy shuddered.

Katherine looked intently down at her hands. "Would he...would he be so very angry, Freddy?"

"Yes," Freddy said honestly. "He'd be devilish angry with me for lying to him, and with you, too, for going along with the lie." He hesitated, then said awkwardly, "You must try to understand, Kate. Ashington is the best of good fellows and my closest friend, but... Well, he's a dashed proud sort. He just couldn't forgive all this deception. Do be careful, won't you? Not to let anyone, particularly Ashington, learn the truth?"

"I shall, Freddy," Kate said wearily. "I promise."

DIANTHA SANK DOWN onto the divan with a sigh. How glad she was to be home! It had been a trying night, with an even more trying morning to follow. Diantha had, despite her fears, slept quite well the night before, in the shed with Henri. She had opened her eyes to find herself in Henri's arms, her head pillowed on the tailor's shoulder. She had awakened before Henri; for a moment or two, she had studied him curiously: the high, intelligent brow, the lips which were slightly lifted in a half smile even in sleep, the strength of his jaw... The blue eyes, brilliant in the morning light.... She had realized that he was awake and jerked back out of his arms. Diantha and Henri had spoken no more of Katherine or Ashington; Henri, true to his word, had intercepted the greengrocer and drawn him off so that Diantha could escape.

Diantha sighed again. It was not until she had left the yard behind the row of shops that she realized she had forgotten her reticule in the shed. Without any money, she had no choice but to walk home, praying fervently that no one she knew would see her on the way. She had almost reached Green Street when Ashington had come swooping down upon her in a closed carriage.

"Well met, Diantha," he had said. For one happy moment Diantha had been exultant, certain here was proof that Ashington still cared for her. That hope had died a quick death when Ashington leaned out of the carriage and almost jerked her inside.

"Ashington!" she had stammered. "I was just...just walking...."

"Don't lie to me, Diantha," he had said coldly.

Diantha had pulled her arm from Ashington's grasp. "Unless I am mistaken, my lord," she had said rigidly, "you no longer have the right to order my whereabouts."

"Nor the desire," Ashington had shot back, "you may be sure of that! Except, that is, when your whereabouts cause your servants to come running to me in a panic, wondering whether you are alive or dead."

"Who came to you? Dorcas?" Diantha had demanded. "I'll turn the ungrateful chit off!"

"You will not," Ashington had said. "Nor will you mistreat her if she is so unwise as to choose to stay with you. I have advised her strongly to leave your employ; I've also offered to help her find another place if she so wishes."

Diantha had gasped in outrage. "Ashington, how could you, when you know what lengths I went to to find her? She's the best maid I've ever had. No one can do hair as she does."

"Then you should not have mistreated her so. She was frantic with worry."

"At least she cared," Diantha had said wildly. "I might just as well be lying dead somewhere, for all you care. And perhaps I shall be!" Diantha had become caught up in the drama of the moment. "Perhaps I shall kill myself, my lord. Would that finally please you?"

"Don't be absurd, Diantha," Ashington had said dampingly. "You won't kill yourself over any man, certainly not over me." He had turned in his seat to look at her and had said, very clearly, "I don't love you, Diantha. We will never be together again. Accept that fact and you will be much happier."

"You must still care," Diantha had blustered. "You shouldn't have come looking for me if you didn't."

"Wrong again, my dear," Ashington had said. "I came out of pity for your maid and nothing more. And I shan't do it again; from now on, if you get yourself into trouble, you will have to get yourself out, too."

"Don't say anything that you'll regret later, Ash," Diantha had retorted. "I know that you're very cross..." She slanted him a seductive look. "Perhaps even a little jealous?"

Ashington sighed. "No, Diantha," he had said. "I am not jealous, not even slightly. What you do is your own affair."

"How can you be so cold?" Diantha had sniffed, peeking at Ashington to watch his reaction. "You've broken my heart!"

"Gammon," he'd replied. "At the very beginning, did we not agree that we should only stay together as long as it amused both of us? And did I not warn you that I had no need or desire to wed? Well?" Diantha had nodded reluctantly. "There you have it, then." He had chuckled a little. "In truth, Di, I do believe it's your pride that I've injured and not your heart." At that moment the carriage had come to a halt before Lady Blandford's door and she had descended, leaving Ashington to drive off without another word.

Diantha shook her head angrily and disposed herself more comfortably on the divan. Her maid entered the drawing room and set a cup of tea down at her mistress's elbow. Diantha glared at Dorcas but said nothing; she had no desire to lose Dorcas, however angry she might be at the servant's impertinence in going to Ashington.

"You have a caller, my lady," Dorcas said quietly. "A gentleman, my lady."

"I don't want to see anyone," Diantha said pettishly. "Who is it?"

"He would not give his name, my lady. He said—"

"I said that I was quite sure you would see me."

Diantha sat bolt upright. "What are *you* doing here?"

Henri smiled at Dorcas. "You may go, my dear," he said kindly. Dorcas looked back and forth between her mistress and Henri, then fled the room without a backward glance.

Diantha was rigid with rage. "Why are you here?" she asked.

Henri dropped his hat and cane on a table and sat down beside Diantha. "I wished to see how you were," he said. "I wanted to be sure that you had come safely home." He reached into his pocket and pulled out Diantha's reticule. "I worried about you, once I realized that you had left this behind. Did you have to walk home?"

"Yes," Diantha said. "Thank you for my reticule. You may go now."

"And no one saw you?" Henri seemed honestly concerned.

Diantha laughed bitterly. "Only Ashington," she said.

"Was he very angry?"

Diantha could feel her eyes filling with tears. "Yes," she said. "He was angry. But not because he was worried about me, or jealous. No, milord Ashington was angry because I had inconvenienced him."

"I'm sorry, *chérie,*" Henri said gently. "I wish that there were something I might do to make you feel better."

"It's all your fault!" Diantha said. "Or rather, that sister of yours—if it weren't for her..."

"You know that to be untrue," Henri said mildly. "Kate has nothing to do with your difficulties with Ashington. It is comfortable to have someone to blame, I know, but in this case..." He shrugged.

"It *is* her fault," said Diantha. "If it weren't for her, Ashington would marry me, I know he would."

Henri shook his head. "I think not," he said. "Ashington is not a gentleman to change his mind, no matter what the subject."

Diantha gasped. "How can you be so cruel?" she cried.

"It is not cruelty, but common sense," Henri said practically. "These Englishmen, they have such strange notions of what is proper and what is not. For myself, I have always been perplexed by this English attitude towards love and marriage. Why would a man not marry a woman whom he knows will please him? The French have a much better understanding of such things, I think."

Diantha seemed dazed by Henri's frank conversation. "Why are you saying these things to me?" she asked.

"Because I pity you," Henri said honestly. "I find it very sad that such a beautiful woman should pursue a man who quite obviously does not want her."

"You don't pity me in the least," Diantha hissed. "Your sister sent you here, didn't she? She thought that you could turn me from my purpose, but she was wrong."

"Kate knows nothing about this," Henri said. "Is it so very hard for you to believe that someone could be interested in your welfare? That someone could care, and be sorry to see you in such distress?"

"You needn't trouble yourself about me; Ashington will come back to me," Diantha said with an assurance she did not feel. "Do you really think that he'll marry your sister over me? I may have been his mistress, but at least I am of his own class!"

Henri rose and took up his hat and cane. "I hope that you may obtain what you so desire, *madame la comtesse*," he said. "But be very careful of what lengths you go to to obtain it. You may well find that the prize is not worth the price."

He turned and walked out of the drawing room, the rigid line of his back clearly displaying his anger. Diantha surprised herself by reaching out a hand towards him; she could barely stop herself from calling out his name. As the door swung shut behind Henri, for one moment Diantha wished miserably that she had never heard of Katherine Crest, Henri L'Ecusson or, for that matter, Lord Ashington.

CHAPTER NINE

LADY HONORIA BASINGSTOKE had, it was generally agreed, outdone herself. The ballroom of her home had been turned into a fairy woodland for Katherine Crest's formal introduction to the ton. Potted trees and flowers had been arranged around the perimeter of the ballroom to create the illusion of a forest glade; the illusion had been extended to the card and supper rooms, where each table was sheltered and made private by a screen of these same flowers and trees. No detail had been overlooked by Honoria in her attempt to create a pastoral setting in her home; she had even gone so far as to have a basket of doves released in the ballroom, to supply a gentle cooing as counterpoint to the music.

The Countess of Blandford surreptitiously scratched her arm and batted a palm frond away from her face. She had made sure to be one of the first guests to arrive and had positioned herself by a group of trees near the entrance to the ballroom. She watched the other guests arriving; each one was greeted by Honoria, then Freddy, then introduced to Katherine. Diantha hoped that Ashington would come soon. If she stood there much longer, she thought, she'd take root herself!

Diantha finally heard Ashington's deep voice greeting Honoria. She was about to step out of the greenery to waylay him when she heard Ashington ask softly, "Is Kate very angry with me, Aunt Honoria?"

"I don't know," Honoria said. "Why would she be?"

"I've come a cropper with her, I fear," Ashington said ruefully. "I was engaged to take Kate driving yesterday morning and completely forgot the appointment."

"Thoughtless," Honoria said. "It's not like you to forget an engagement. What happened?"

"Oh, one of those unpleasant obligations that one is sometimes subject to," Ashington said. "Tiresome, but unavoidable."

Diantha could feel a flush washing up her face. She clenched her fists, about to burst forth from her hiding place, when a strong hand gripped her arm and pulled her away from the quartet at the entrance.

"Temper, temper, my dear Diantha," said a languid voice in her ear. "I beg you, this one time, think before you speak."

Diantha rounded on her companion. "Do you spend quite all your time sneaking up on people, Keswick?" she hissed.

"Only on you, my dear," Lord Keswick said amiably. "But then, you are so very imperceptive, aren't you?" Diantha turned to walk away, but Keswick forestalled her. "Hold, Diantha," he said. "You and I must talk."

"I cannot think," Diantha ground out, "what we should have to talk about."

"Ashington," said Keswick. "And Miss Crest."

"I'll stand no more ridicule from you, Kes," Diantha warned him.

"As ridicule is the farthest thing from my mind," he answered, "that should not be a problem. Shall we?" He held out his arm. After a moment's hesitation, Diantha took it.

"I have decided, my love, that it would be a very good thing indeed if you were to wed Ashington," Keswick said.

"How very kind of you, my lord," Diantha said angrily. "I am most flattered, I promise you!"

"Come down off your high ropes," Keswick advised her. "If we put our heads together, I believe that we may do the thing."

"I don't need your help."

Keswick cocked a brow at her. "Really?" he said. "I heard Ashington talking just now; can you enjoy being referred to as an unpleasant necessity?" Diantha gaped at him. "You needn't look so amazed, Diantha," he went on. "Your face told all. I don't know what brought you two together yesterday, but 'tis clear it wasn't romance."

"Ashington did me a service," Diantha mumbled.

"Well, then, you must go and thank him for it, as prettily as you may," Keswick said. "Instead of railing at him like a guttersnipe, exert your not inconsiderable charm, my dear." He paused, then added, "And you might make sure that Miss Crest knows that Ashington was with you, while she was sitting at home waiting for him."

"Why are you being so helpful of a sudden?" Diantha asked.

"Suffice it to say, my dear girl, that for the moment at least, our interests march together."

"AND THIS IS Mr. Edwin Rankin," Freddy said. "Edwin, my cousin, Miss Katherine Crest."

Lady Rankin tittered. "Oh, you needn't introduce my son to this beautiful young lady," she said. "They met at my ball and are well on the way to becoming fast friends. Is that not so, Edwin?"

Edwin Rankin bowed and pressed a wet kiss onto Katherine's hand. "Indeed," he stammered. "That is to say, we met at my mother's ball. Do you remember me, Miss Crest?"

"But of course she does, Edwin," Lady Rankin said. "Must you be so foolish?" She turned to a bewildered Katherine. "Now, my dear, you must promise to save a dance for my Edwin. He'd be quite heartbroken if you didn't; that's all he's been talking about the whole day. Isn't it, Edwin?" Edwin Rankin blinked and nodded his head nervously. Out of the corner of her eye, Katherine could see Ashington speaking to Honoria, but she refused to acknowledge his presence. She smiled brilliantly at Edwin Rankin, promising to save him a country dance.

"There, now," said Lady Rankin with satisfaction as she led her son away. "I told you that you could do the pretty if you just put your mind to it. Did you see how she smiled at you?"

Behind them, Ashington had stepped up to Katherine. "Kate," he began. "I—"

"My lord," said Katherine with an infinitesimal nod. "How kind of you to grace us with your presence." Her tone could not have been colder.

Freddy stared at her, open mouthed. "Kate!" he whispered. "What are you doing?"

Katherine ignored her cousin's protest and pointedly turned her attention to the next couple in line.

Freddy's face had paled at Katherine's incivility, but he said gamely, "You must forgive her, Ash. She's not feeling quite the thing. Headache, don't you know."

"Oh, no, Freddy, it's not that," Honoria said helpfully. "She's angry because—"

"Never mind, Aunt Honoria," Ash said stiffly. "It is of no moment." He turned and walked away.

Freddy shook his head and tugged on Katherine's sleeve. "What's got into you, Kate?" he asked, quietly enough that only Katherine could hear. "That was horribly rude, you know."

Katherine ignored his question. "We have guests to greet, Freddy," she reminded him. Freddy hesitated, then shrugged and presented the next person in line to Katherine.

Automatically, Katherine bowed and smiled, curtsied and nodded, but all the while her heart was pounding in her ears. How dared Ashington stand there and speak to her as though nothing had happened, as though he had not deeply insulted her? She was amazed that he had had the gall to come this evening, after what he had done. And Freddy had called *her* rude! But despite her anger, a voice in her head persisted in making excuses for Ashington. What if he had been unavoidably detained? What if something had happened that made it impossible for him to come? He might have sent a message, Katherine told herself firmly. But what if he had not been able to? Katherine could not help but sigh. How very difficult it was, she thought, to stay properly angry with my Lord Ashington!

"Now, what has made you look so very sad, my dear?"

Katherine blinked; Lord Keswick looked solemnly down at her.

"My—my lord," she said. "Pray forgive me; I was wool-gathering, I fear. You startled me."

He sighed. "Yes, I do seem to have that effect on ladies," he said. "I begin to think that I should wear a bell round my neck, like a cow, to let the fairer sex know when I am coming."

"How absurd you are, my lord," Katherine said. She did not smile.

Keswick took one of her hands. "Won't you tell me what's troubling you?" he asked.

Katherine essayed a weak smile. "It's nothing," she said. "Only a fit of the megrims."

"Well, then, let me jolly you out of it," he suggested, tucking her arm under his. "I have been reliably informed that I am quite absurd."

"But I must greet our guests," Katherine said.

"Oh, I'm sure that Lady Basingstoke can spare you. Almost everyone has arrived, I think; they won't miss you. Lady Basingstoke! May I whisk Miss Crest away for a little refreshment?"

Honoria considered Katherine's unhappy expression for a moment, then nodded. "Run along, my dear," she said. "Enjoy yourself."

Katherine had no choice but to agree. Keswick led her off into the crowd.

"I could not help but notice the way you greeted Lord Ashington," Keswick said. "It is bad of you to quarrel with him, you know, when he is the *raison d'être* for this entire affair." A wave of his hand indicated the ballroom, the partygoers and the orchestra playing at the end of the chamber.

Determined not to let Ashington spoil her enjoyment, Katherine spoke as lightly as she could. "I think you must be mistaken, my lord."

"My dear child!" Keswick looked at her. "Can it be that you haven't realized? I would wager any sum you'd care to name that Lady Basingstoke planned this soirée for the sole purpose of putting you in Ashington's way. She's decided that you'd do very nicely as a wife for his lordship."

"That's ridiculous," Katherine said, hating herself for the colour that she could feel staining her cheeks. "I barely know him."

"Perhaps Lady Basingstoke is hoping that love will strike like lightning. It can happen that way, you know," Keswick said. "I am living proof of it." Katherine looked away in confusion; he patted her hand. "There, I've embarrassed you, haven't I?" he said easily. "Put it out of your mind, my dear. Just remember that if you ever stand in need of a friend, I am here. Now, let us perambulate! We must at very least pretend to enjoy the entertainment that Honoria has been kind enough to arrange for us."

ASHINGTON STRODE BLINDLY through Honoria's ballroom. How could she? he asked himself angrily. How could Katherine Crest humiliate him in front of his friends? Why, the chit had the manners of a shop-girl. Certainly it had been rude of him, the previous day, not to send her word that he had been delayed, but that was no excuse for her behaviour. He had a good mind to go back and tell her so, right to her face; that would be serving her her just deserts. But unlike Kate, he told himself, he had better manners than to cause such a scene!

Diantha caught up to Ashington by the simple expedient of almost running until she was close enough to call his name. "Ash!" Ashington turned round and scowled at her.

"What do you want, Diantha?" he asked curtly.

"Why, nothing in particular," she said, smiling up at him. "Just to say hello, and to pass the time of day."

"Hello," Ashington said.

"Surely you can summon up just a little more civility than that, Ash," she said. "I know we are no longer special friends, but might we not be ordinary friends?" She tucked her arm through his. "You know, the sort who stroll together and animadvert on the deplorable state of the country and bewail the general decline of trade?"

As Diantha had never before shown a hint of interest in politics or trade, Ashington was obliged to laugh, but he did not weaken. "I think not," he said. "I'm quite sure that you can find any number of gentlemen who would be thrilled to discuss any subject at all with you."

"Let me be honest, then," Diantha said disarmingly. "I've given a great deal of thought to what you said yesterday. I understand that you do not wish to continue our liaison. Really, I do! I'm sorry if I've been, well, unpleasant."

"There's no need for apologies, Diantha, as long as you remember what I said. I meant every word of it."

"I know that, Ash," Diantha said humbly.

"Is that all?" Ashington was still wary.

"I wanted to ask you a favour," Diantha said. "No, you needn't look so alarmed. It's a simple thing."

"I don't think—"

"At least let me ask you," Diantha said. "That won't hurt, will it?" She smiled up at Ashington. "You'll think me mad, I know, but I wondered if you would be so kind as to take me in to the supper room."

"Why?" Ashington asked suspiciously.

Diantha shrugged. "'Tis wicked of me, but I wish to give all the gossipmongers something to think about. You must know that there has been a certain amount of talk about our... separation. One or two of the old tabbies have used the subject to be somewhat unkind to me."

"I'm sorry to hear that, Diantha, but..." Ashington began awkwardly.

"But I should be used to it?" Diantha finished lightly. "I know, I should. But I'm human enough to wish to get a little of my own back. And wouldn't they be surprised, to see the two of us stroll in together?" She held a hand up solemnly. "I swear to you, I'll attach no undue importance to your kindness, if you do grant me this favour." Diantha read his face and added carefully, "Of course, if you think that Miss Crest might be offended..."

Ashington frowned. "What has Miss Crest to say to the matter?"

Diantha tried to look innocent. "Well, there are those who seem to think that you've an interest there," she said. "I shouldn't wish to cause any trouble between you and Miss Crest, if that is the case. These very young girls do tend to take offence rather easily."

If that wasn't the outside of enough! Ashington thought. After the way Kate had treated him... "Nonsense," he said, tucking Diantha's arm more firmly into his own. "As long as you understand that this is just a favour, without significance, then I daresay it would do no harm. And I have a grievance or two against the gossipers, myself."

"I do understand," said Diantha meekly. "I know that whatever we once had is finished. I may not like it, but I do accept it." She sighed. "Ah, well," she said, "this is not the first time I've been given my *congé* and I doubt it will be the last."

Ashington regarded Diantha with a strange look in his eyes. "Diantha, do you mind if I ask you something?"

"How did I ever get started on my notorious career?" Diantha supplied calmly. "I'm sure you know most of the story, Ash; how I was married very young and also widowed and left destitute very young. What could I do? I tried looking for another husband, but no one would bother with a penniless widow, even if she was the daughter of a duke and the goddaughter of a prince. The choice at the time seemed to be between sin and starvation. Starvation held no appeal for me, whereas sin... !" She smiled, and Ashington was reminded of her deeply sensual nature. "It seemed a fair trade at the time," she concluded. "A life of gaiety and some pleasure, for my good name."

"And how does it seem to you now?" Ashington realized that this was the first real conversation he had ever had with his former mistress; the realization made him feel ashamed.

Diantha shrugged. "'Tis far too late to repine," she said pragmatically. Over the potted trees which surrounded the supper room, she saw Keswick's head, bent down to speak to someone; he looked over at her and gave a tiny nod of his head. Diantha manoeuvred Ashington until they were standing on the other side of the trees from Keswick and his companion.

"But how unmannerly of me, Ash," she said, her voice raised a little. "I've quite forgotten to thank you for your services to me yesterday. It meant the world to me that you cared enough to come. I'll never forget it."

"Just as long as you understand that—" Ashington began.

"There is no one that I can rely on as I rely on you," Diantha interrupted. "With you as my protector, Ash, I need never worry." She turned and led Ashington towards the other side of the supper room.

"I am not your protector, Diantha; be very sure of that," Ashington said as they walked away.

Inside the supper room, Katherine's hand stiffened on Keswick's arm and she had all she could do to stifle her gasp of outrage. She had not heard Ashington's final comment.

"Miss Crest...Katherine...are you well?" Keswick asked, much satisfied. "You look pale."

Katherine shook her head, unable to speak. *Protector*, she fumed silently. Ashington was so lost to what was proper that he had left Katherine dangling while he dallied with his mistress, and yet had the effrontery to call Keswick a rake! The laughable thing was that she had actually begun to think that she had wronged Ashington. The more fool she! Whatever attraction Lord Ashington had once held for her was dead, she told herself, as dead as his lordship's honour.

CHAPTER TEN

"Ash! I've been looking all over Town for you."
Freddy Basingstoke dropped into a chair. "Where
have you been?"

"Right here, Freddy," Ashington said. He gestured at the famous bow window of White's Club.
"Just sitting and watching the world go by."

"And drinking, by the looks of it," Freddy said,
eyeing the half empty bottle of brandy which stood on
the table between them. He looked round. "Do you
know, I'd no notion that White's was open so early in
the day. I don't believe I've ever set foot in the clubs
before noon; not until now, that is."

"It's not early, Freddy, it's late," Ashington said.
Freddy noticed that his friend was still wearing the
impeccably tailored black frock coat and knee
breeches he had had on the night before.

"What, haven't you been home yet?" Freddy exclaimed. "What ho, old friend? It's not like you to be
out all night. Is something wrong?"

Ashington did not answer. He gestured curtly at a
waiter and watched the man place a glass in front of
Freddy. Ashington filled it.

"I see," said Freddy, watching Ashington closely. "It must be a woman. Diantha?"

"Actually, Diantha is behaving most reasonably...for Diantha," Ashington said. "But what makes you think it's a lady that's troubling me, Fred? Am I so notorious a womanizer?"

"No, but it stands to reason," Freddy said. "When a man sits drinking brandy at ten o'clock in the morning, with such a look on his face, it can only be a female, that's all."

Ashington raised his glass to his friend. "For once you are quite correct," he said. "It *is* a woman. The most stubborn, unreasonable, prickly..." He tossed back the rest of his brandy. "To the devil with her!" he said. "Why should I even concern myself with what she thinks?"

"It appears that you have good reason to," Freddy said.

"What? Why?"

"Well, I don't know who this female is, but if she's got you this upset, Ash, it seems to me you must care for her," Freddy said practically.

Ashington snorted. "You're mad," he said.

"No, but think, Ash!" Freddy said. "I've never seen you give a second thought to a woman; even Diantha never made you so angry. She might have irritated you, or annoyed you, but she never reduced you to a state like this. Only two emotions ever made a man behave so: love or hate. Do you hate this woman?"

"No," Ashington was bound to admit.

"All right, then," Freddy said triumphantly. "You must love her."

Ashington shook his head. "A pretty theory, Freddy, but untrue. At this moment, given the choice between throttling her and making love to her, I would most definitely opt for the throttling."

Freddy looked even more smug. "That just proves my point." He leaned forward. "Who is she, Ash?" he asked. "Some new beauty whom you've discovered?"

"No!" Ashington snapped, then added, "Well, yes, she is beautiful, I suppose, but...beauty is as beauty does," he finished lamely. Freddy laughed. Ashington said irritably, "Oh, to the devil with you, Freddy! Must you plague me with your half-baked theories? Why were you looking for me?"

Freddy sobered. "I wanted to apologize to you for Kate's behaviour last night," he said awkwardly. "Truthfully, Ash, I can't think what got into her. But you won't hold it against her, will you?"

"Miss Crest," said Ashington coldly, "appears to have no great regard for my opinion of her."

"Oh, but that's not true, Ash," Freddy said earnestly. "She's very fond of you, I know she is. And I shouldn't wish... That is to say... I hope you shan't..." He stopped.

"Shan't what?" Ashington asked.

"Shan't, well, turn against her, or give her the cut direct," Freddy said. "It would ruin her. You're such a pink of the ton that everyone would follow your lead if you weren't kind to Kate."

Ashington stared at his friend. "Well, I like that," he said in disgust. "What kind of an oaf do you think me, Freddy? Do you imagine I'd ruin a slip of a girl, only because she was less than welcoming?"

Freddy sighed with relief. "I knew you wouldn't, Ash, only you did look so very furious last night! And I'll speak to Kate about it, honestly I will. She must be made to understand that such behaviour is not *comme il faut.*"

"Don't trouble yourself," Ashington said. "I'm sure you were quite right when you said it was only the headache."

"It's good of you to be so understanding," Freddy said. He caught sight of a clock on the mantelpiece and rose to his feet. "I'm off," he said cheerfully. "Aunt Honoria wants me to escort her to some old crony's house. It'll be the devil of a bore, but what is one to do?" As he started to leave the table he turned back for one parting shot. "Remember what I said, Ash," he said with a grin. "Love or hate, m'boy; love or hate!"

KATHERINE SAT HUDDLED in the depths of a winged armchair, feet curled up beneath her. She shivered as she heard the thunder cracking outside and let the book she had been pretending to read slip from her fingers. In the week since her ball, she had been unable to shake off the cloud of depression which engulfed her. A hundred times she turned her mind resolutely away from Ashington, but to no avail. She found herself thinking about him constantly, wondering what he was doing, wondering if he was with Diantha. It would have been better if she and Ashington had never met, she thought. If she could have kept her dreams intact—the dreams she had dreamed watching him from the window when he entered or left her brother's shop. They had been the fantasies of a child, she realized now. Because he was tall and handsome, she had thought him noble and good, too. What a fool she had been! Her time spent moving among the ton had opened her eyes; gentlemen were treacherous and unreliable, and, left to herself, she would have had nothing more to do with any of them.

But she was not the only affected party, unfortunately. Maman had not worked and saved for years so that Katherine could mope about Freddy's house, indulging in a fit of the dismals, Katherine told herself firmly. She could not bear the thought of disappointing her mother so. After hearing the sad story of Marie's life, so full of tragedy and disappointment, Katherine vowed that she would not be the one to dash her mother's final hopes. She was here to find herself a well-born husband, and find one she would.

As if on cue, Honoria's butler entered the room. "My lord Keswick, Miss Katherine," he said, and bowed Keswick into the room.

"My lord," said Katherine, hastily pulling her feet from beneath her. "I had not expected you." She looked down, realized that her feet were still bare and blushed in confusion.

Keswick's blue eyes gleamed. "Allow me," he said, and crossed the room swiftly to kneel before her. He took one foot in his hands and gently ran a slender finger along the curve of her instep. Katherine shivered. "You have beautiful feet," he said softly. "Almost as beautiful as the rest of you." Gently he smoothed the thin stocking she wore, caressing each toe in turn; he bent his head and kissed each pink toenail, before sliding her slipper slowly onto her foot. "Shall I stop?" he asked.

Katherine felt a delicious warmth steal over her. "I—I..." she stammered.

How easy this was going to be, Keswick thought delightedly. Whatever his detractors might say about him, no one had ever questioned his ability with the ladies, or his mastery of the art of seduction. He chuckled deep in his throat and repeated his actions with her other foot, the caresses more languorous, the kisses more prolonged. When at last the second slipper was on her foot, he leaned back on his heels and looked up at her.

"You must know why I've come," he said.

Katherine could not answer him. For one moment, as his warm breath had touched her skin and she had felt the softness of his lips, she had imagined it was Ashington's dark head that was bent over her foot. She felt ashamed.

"I love you, Kate," he said. "I want you to marry me." He rose and stood before her. "Despite my reputation, I have never asked any lady to be my bride. I was waiting, though I knew it not. Waiting for you, my dear."

Katherine leapt to her feet. "My lord!" she said. "I do not know...that is to say..."

He put his hands on her shoulders. "I know that you do not love me," he said. He took her hand. "But I think—" he pressed a kiss against her palm "—that you might learn to." He kissed the pulse that fluttered wildly at the inside of her wrist. "Don't you?"

"I—I..."

Keswick led Katherine to a divan and sat down beside her. "Don't be frightened," he said. "Tell me what you feel."

Katherine clasped her hands tightly together. All of a sudden she knew that she could not marry Keswick, or any other gentleman, without telling him of her background. Katherine would never have believed, before her introduction to the ton, the artifice and lack of honesty to be found in Polite Society. No one told the truth; not even Ashington, as his conversation with Diantha had so clearly demonstrated. Katherine realized now that, whatever the consequences, she must tell Keswick her story. "Before you go any further, my lord, there is something which you should know...."

Without further preamble, Katherine launched into the story of her life. As she began to speak, Keswick toyed with the black hair which fell down her back.

When she reached the point in the story where Marie's maid was struck down, his hand stilled; had she been looking at him, she would have seen his eyes grow wide with disbelief.

This was Cousin Henry's child? he thought, stunned. Henry had actually married the chit he had seemed so taken with that day, the day the young Keswick, driving so wildly, had struck down that dashed peasant in the street? The French girl had been a nuisance, wailing and crying, calling Keswick a murderer. Henry had jumped down from the curricle to comfort the girl and had had the impertinence to join her in castigating Keswick; Keswick had never seen his cousin after that day. He had known that Henry married badly. Henry's father had cast his son off, and there had been no further communication between his cousin and his family. But somehow Keswick thought that Henry had left the country. Certainly he had never had any notion that his cousin had had a family, or that Henry had turned to trade to support them.

A chilling thought struck him. Did Ashington know of the girl's birth and upbringing? Keswick thought not. If Ashington had known Katherine's story, he would not have wasted a moment in using the information to humiliate Keswick. And the story would humiliate him, Keswick realized; half the ton would scorn him for having a cousin in trade, and the other half would revile him for allowing members of his own family to live in what amounted to penury. Keswick knew that his reputation could not stand another smirch. He was tolerated by the ton because of his birth and breeding, but one more scandal might be enough to ruin him forever. It took every ounce of his self-control to stifle the bitter laugh which rose to his lips. Katherine had trapped him, as neatly as any doxy on the hunt for a husband. Despite their quarrel, Keswick knew that Ashington was drawn to Katherine; did Keswick not wed his cousin, Ashington might offer for her, and the fool girl would blurt out her story, just as she had to him. There had been some talk about Keswick at the time of the accident and Ashington would be sure to remember it. He would not be long, if the girl told him her story, in realizing that Keswick's own cousin had been Katherine's father. And what would Ashington do with the story, with the twin spurs of hatred for Keswick and embarrassment at having pursued a shopgirl? It did not bear thinking of.

"So you see, my lord, I could not let you honour me with a proposal of marriage without telling you the truth," Katherine finished. "I could not live with myself if I had."

"It matters not to me," said Keswick smoothly, giving no indication of the hatred and turmoil which filled him. "I love you, Kate. My offer stands."

Katherine squeezed his hand. "I always knew that the evil people attributed to you was false," she said gratefully. "Your goodness overwhelms me."

"But what is your answer, my love?" Keswick feigned an ardour he did not feel; the sight of the young lady he now knew to be his cousin filled him with disgust. "Say only that you will be mine. Say yes, dearest Kate!"

"Give me time, my lord," Katherine asked. "Only a little while, to reflect. Then I shall answer you."

Keswick agreed solemnly, assuring Katherine that he would wait with bated breath for her answer, all the while thinking, "You will marry me, my girl. By hook, crook, or stile, you will marry me!"

HENRI L'ECUSSON STOOD beneath the dripping trees and turned his collar up against the weather. *Just like a woman,* he thought disgustedly, *late, and in a dashed thunderstorm!* He grinned wryly; he should have listened to Maman. She had warned him that it would rain, that morning when he was leaving the shop. Her bones told her, she had said, and they were never wrong. Henri winced as a bolt of lightning split the sky, and he moved closer to the trees, seeking shelter. She probably wasn't coming. It would show remarkable good sense on her part, more sense than Henri thought she had, if she did stay at home in such weather.

He heard a whinny and, straining to see through the rain, caught sight of a small, bedraggled figure leading a limping horse.

"*Mon Dieux,* Diantha, you're drenched," he said, pulling her underneath the trees. "Why did you not stay at home?"

Diantha's teeth were chattering with cold. "I needed to see you, as I said in my note," she told him.

"I am overwhelmed by the honour you do me, my lady, but I might wish that you had chosen a better day for it," he said, and smiled down at her.

"What do you find so amusing?" Diantha snapped.

"You," Henri said. His smile broadened. "If your friends could but see the elegant Countess of Bland-ford now...!"

Diantha pushed her sodden curls, limp with rain, out of her eyes. "They would not find me half so comical," she snarled, "as they will your sister when they find out who she really is." Diantha tossed her head. "But of course they won't find it amusing at all, will they, to think that a little shopgirl has been fool-ing them."

Henri's brows snapped together, all traces of amusement gone. "You will not tell," he said. "We have agreed to that."

"Well, I've changed my mind," Diantha said sul-lenly. "That is what I wanted to tell you. I have de-cided that it will not suit me at all to be silent."

Henri's brow cleared. "You are only angry," he said with some relief. "Angry that you are wet, and that I laughed at you." He took her hand. "I'm sorry," he said gently. "I was only teasing you."

Diantha turned away from him. "But I *am* going to tell," she said harshly. Around them the storm raged; wind tore through the trees and thunder echoed across the wide reaches of the park.

"Why?"

"You must understand...I have to," she said, amazed to hear the pleading tone in her own voice. "I won't let Ashington just throw me over. I can't!"

Henri stared at her. "You know, then," he said.

"Know what?" Diantha was confused.

"That my lord Ashington is in love with my sister," Henri said gently.

Diantha could feel the blood rushing into her face. "You're mad," she said. "And how would you know it if he were?"

"You must remember, *ma chère,* that though I am not of your world, I do still inhabit its fringes," Henri said. "My gentlemen talk as I fit them, and I listen. Ashington loves Katherine."

Diantha knew that it was true. It was this knowledge which had made her realize the folly of trying to win Ashington back with soft words and ready smiles. She would never be able to charm Ash back into her life; he would never even notice her, for his attention was all for Katherine.

Henri read Diantha's face. "You knew it," he said.

"All the more reason for me to tell," Diantha said desperately. "It's the only way for me to have a chance with Ash."

Henri stepped closer to Diantha. "Are you so sure that you want another chance?" he asked softly.

"Of course I do," Diantha said, but not as vehemently as she might have wished.

"Stop and consider the matter, my lady," Henri said. "You send me an urgent command to meet you, you ride here through a veritable downpour, and for what? Only to tell me that you will ruin my sister. You didn't need to tell me," he pointed out. "You might just as easily have gone ahead and done it."

"I, er, only thought it fair," Diantha said, then added hastily, "What other reason could I possibly have for wanting to see you?"

"I am a man, *chérie,* and you are a woman." Diantha could not tear her eyes away from the deep cerulean of Henri's gaze. "Whatever we are in life, everything comes back to that one basic fact. Does it not?"

Diantha could feel her knees beginning to tremble. "Pray do not be absurd," she said. "And don't call me *chérie!* You haven't the right; you're only a tailor."

"A tailor, perhaps, but a man none the less," Henri said. He took Diantha's hand and placed it against his coat. "Do you feel my heart, *chérie?*" he asked softly.

Diantha could feel the pounding of Henri's heart through the superfine of his frock coat. For one moment, she was transported back to the greengrocer's shed, her head against Henri's shoulder, his strong body stretched out beside her.

"You do feel it, don't you?" Henri whispered. "Feel it!"

Diantha's eyes closed; despite the rain, she felt a delicious warmth stealing through her. She shivered.

Instantly Henri was all concern. "Are you cold, *ma petite?*" he asked. "Come, let me share my cloak with you." He held his arm wide, the edge of the cloak spread to receive Diantha.

"No!" she said. She looked away from Henri and tried to steady her voice. "I must go."

"Very well," Henri raised her hand to his lips. "And you will not, of course, say anything about Katherine."

"No...yes...I don't know," Diantha said. She felt dazed.

"Thank you, *ma chérie.*" Henri reached out for Diantha.

Diantha turned and seized the bridle of her horse. "But I shall still have Ashington, Henri," Diantha cried. "I shall!" She flung herself into the saddle and galloped away.

Henri looked after her, a slight smile twisting his lips. "Will you, *ma petite?*" he asked aloud. "Will you indeed?"

CHAPTER ELEVEN

ASHINGTON REINED IN his horse and took a deep breath of the fresh spring air. The previous day's storm had washed the air clean and left the grass glistening in the morning sun. This was his favourite time of day to ride, early, before the Park became crowded with ladies and gentlemen of the ton, anxious to see and be seen. Only the groundskeepers were out and about at this hour, carefully manicuring the green sweep of lawn and tending the flowers which filled the Park with fragrance. One or two of them nodded and touched their hats to Ashington; his lordship was a familiar sight to them.

Ashington tapped his horse's flanks and wondered if he dared venture to gallop. Such energetic riding was frowned upon in Town, the powers that be having declared that such enthusiasm was ill-bred. He decided reluctantly that it would not be wise, though the thought of a hard, head-clearing gallop held much appeal for him this morning.

Ashington had not slept well the night before. He had tossed and turned in his bed, Freddy's words echoing in his mind; *Love or hate, m'boy, love or hate!* First he had been angry, telling himself that Freddy was a fool and not to be heeded; then he had wondered, wondered if perhaps there was some truth in what Freddy had said. Ashington had attempted to understand his own feelings for Miss Katherine Crest, but he could make no sense of them. All he knew was that he did have feelings for the girl, and that those feelings were not hatred.

Ashington rounded a stand of trees and slowed his horse to a walk. Across the velvety sward he saw another early rider, a lady, mounted on a powerful and showy roan stallion. The lady drooped in her saddle; every line of her body seemed to radiate sadness and dismay. Ashington took another look, then spurred his mount and galloped across to her.

"Katherine . . . Kate! Is anything wrong?"

Katherine jerked herself erect in the saddle. "No," she replied in a small voice. "I'm quite well, my lord, thank you."

Ashington was examining Katherine's horse. "Whatever possessed you to take out Freddy's stallion?" he said. "It's far too powerful a mount for a lady; you might have been killed!" He looked about sharply. "And where is your groom?"

Katherine lifted her head. "I wished to ride alone this morning," she said. "Your concern does you credit, my lord, but I assure you, there is no need for it. Good day." She lifted her hands, but Ashington reached out and grabbed her bridle.

"I'll see you home," he said.

"There is no reason—"

"There is every reason in the world," Ashington said. "I should be the greatest cad imaginable if I let you go on alone. And Freddy would never forgive me."

Katherine opened her mouth as if to speak, then closed it again. Short of slashing Ashington with her crop, she saw no hope of escape, so, with a stiff bow of her head she acquiesced, and the pair began to canter across the grass.

Ashington slid a look at the girl out of the corner of his eye. Katherine sat the horse as though she were nailed on, her gaze fixed firmly on the horizon. "I'm sorry I left you waiting that day," he said. "I was unavoidably detained."

"Ah, yes," Katherine drawled. "Busy with Lady Blandford, I daresay?" The minute the words were spoken she gasped and clapped a gloved hand over her mouth.

Ashington stared at Katherine. "I beg your pardon?"

"I—I..." Katherine stammered, then gulped. "I'm sorry," she said in a small voice. She was appalled at her own temerity, but not surprised by it; her heart had spoken, not her head. All along, she realized, it had been Ashington; her heart had been his before they had ever met, and always would be. The realization did not raise Katherine's spirits, but made them plummet even lower. What hope had she with Ashington?

"I wish I had never come here," she cried. "This world...*your* world," she said accusingly, "is full of lies and hypocrisy. I want to go home." She raised a hand to her eyes and Ashington realized she was wiping tears away.

"Kate," he said, and pulled her horse into a grove of trees. "Please, my dear, don't cry." At the sound of Ashington's kind words, all Katherine's self-control deserted her and she slumped over the neck of her horse, weeping.

"Kate, don't," he begged her. His feeling of tenderness for the girl overwhelmed him; he had not known it possible to feel so protective towards anyone, or so cut by another's unhappiness. He slipped from the saddle and held out his arms to her. "I can't properly comfort you while you're on horseback," he said with the shadow of a smile. "Come; we'll walk, and you may tell me what is wrong." Katherine said nothing, so Ashington added gently, "Don't be afraid, Kate; I promise you, whatever it is, I shall stand your friend and help you."

Katherine looked down at her love and knew that her feelings were not entirely unreciprocated. Her heart leapt in her chest. Was it possible? Could it be that he did love her, and would understand? Was it possible that they might find their happiness together?

"Please, my dear," Ashington coaxed with a smile. "Do you wish me to be thought the veriest bully? It

will do my reputation no good, you know, to be seen
haranguing a weeping woman.''

His reputation! Katherine's hope died stillborn.
What a fool she had been, to think for even a moment that she and Ashington might be together. If her
secret came out it would mean ruin for Ashington, she
realized. He, who had been lionized by the ton, would
be shunned by them if he married so far beneath him.

''I must go,'' she blurted out, and drove her heels
into her mount's flanks. Ashington could only stare
after her in amazement. By the time he jumped back
into his own saddle, she was gone.

DIANTHA, COUNTESS of Blandford, unpinned the
brooch from the low-cut bosom of her satin gown and
tossed it onto the table. ''This should cover it, I
think,'' she said. She, Edwin Rankin and his friend
Ingham were seated at a gaming table in one of the
small, exclusive gaming hells of Portman Square. The
room was filled with the fumes of tobacco smoke and
brandy; the three had been there all night, playing pi-
quet.

Edwin Rankin tossed his cards on the table. ''Too
rich for my blood, I fear,'' he said. ''I'm through; I've
lost a king's ransom already. You've the devil's own
luck tonight, Ingham.''

''Well, Diantha?'' said Ingham.

The countess spread her cards, face up, on the table. ''My hand, I believe, Ingham,'' she said smugly.
She reached out to rake in her winnings.

"I think not," Ingham said. He displayed his own cards.

"By Jupiter, Ingham, you've done it again," said Edwin. He turned to Diantha. "You never should have bid him up, you know. It's plain to see that it's his night. He can't lose!" Edwin rose from his seat and crossed the room to push back one of the heavy velvet draperies which covered the windows at the end of the room. "Why, it's full light out," he said in surprise. "Time for me to go, and past. My mother has no doubt bullied the servants into telling her what time I get in, and I don't particularly relish the thought of spending the rest of the day being interrogated about where, and with whom, I was."

Ingham, too, rose from the table. "I'll join you, Edwin," he said.

Diantha's hand shot out and grabbed Ingham by the wrist. "Not while you're winning," she said with a thin smile. "'Twould be most unmannerly of you not to give me the opportunity to win back a little of my money."

Ingham looked down at Diantha, his expression carefully blank. "You have nothing left to wager with," he pointed out to the countess.

Diantha's eyebrows shot up. "But you will accept my vowels, of course?" she said, making the question a statement.

Edwin snorted. "Ingham would be mad to do any such thing," he said frankly. "You're pockets-to-let, Di, and we all know it."

Diantha flushed. "Shut up, Edwin," she said.

"Well, I like that!" Edwin Rankin said, offended. "I'm only saying what everyone in Town knows. You've not a sou to your name, Diantha. Can you deny it?"

Diantha ignored his question, turning her attention back to Ingham. "Are you saying that you won't accept my vowels, my sworn promise to pay?" she asked him.

"It's late, Diantha," Ingham said. "Perhaps it would be as well..."

"It would be as well, sir," interrupted Diantha furiously, "for you to do the honourable thing and allow me my chance to recoup my losses. If you won't trust me for the money, perhaps I might remind you that my lord Ashington has always made good my losses in the past. He will do the same now, you need have no fear."

Edwin Rankin gave a cackle of laughter. "Now, there, Di, you're fair and far out!" he said. "We all know that Ashington has given you your *congé*."

"Edwin..." Ingham said warningly.

"But you know it's true, Ingham," Edwin protested. "Ashington wouldn't lift a hand to help Diantha now."

Diantha sucked in her breath. "Rankin," she said in an awful voice, "I don't know where you've got this absurd notion, but I assure you, Ashington and I are as close as ever we were."

"No, you're not," Edwin said. "Do you think me a fool? All of London knows that Ashington has a tendre for La Crest and that it's only a matter of time until they become betrothed. Are you asking me to believe that Ashington would be proposing to Miss Crest on the one hand and dallying with you on the other? I'm not such a flat as all that. Ashington ain't the type for that sort of havey-cavey behaviour."

"Why, you... You..." Diantha was speechless with rage.

Ingham seized Edwin Rankin by the arm. "You've said quite enough, Edwin," he said grimly. "I bid you good night, Diantha." He pulled Rankin out the door.

Diantha jumped to her feet and stormed about the room. So "everyone" knew, did they? That Crest chit had made a laughing-stock of her, and among her own friends and acquaintances! Diantha's face burned at the thought of the things Edwin Rankin had said and at the notion that such a fool as Rankin should dare to laugh at her. *Well, let him laugh!* she thought, snatching up her cloak and reticule. *Let them all laugh.* Whatever happened, Lord Ashington would not marry Katherine Crest. Diantha would see to that.

In a white-hot blaze of anger, Diantha stopped for nothing but a quick change of clothing on her way to Freddy Basingstoke's Town house. As soon as Croaker, Freddy's butler, had announced her, Diantha marched into Freddy's drawing room.

"Good morning, my lady," said Katherine, smoothing the skirts of her blue muslin frock as she rose. She held out a hand to her caller. "How lovely you look." Katherine's tone was wistful; she had to admit, despite her prejudice, that Diantha was a gloriously beautiful woman.

"Why, thank you, my dear," said Diantha, pulling off her gloves as she settled down beside Katherine. "You are quite in looks yourself today; that frock is stunning." She paused. "Did your brother make it?"

The colour drained from Katherine's face. "What?" she whispered.

"I said, did your brother make that gown?" Diantha repeated. "I know that Henri is more familiar with gentleman's clothing, but I'm sure he could turn his hand to women's attire with just as much success. And think what a savings it would be! The more popular modistes are frightfully dear, are they not?"

Katherine felt a curious sense of unreality, as though she had stepped from waking into a dream. "How did you find out?" she asked.

Diantha shrugged gracefully. "Surely you did not think to fool us all forever?" she said. "Despite its size, London is, in many ways, like a small village. Everything is known in the end." Diantha was not enjoying her revenge as much as she had thought she would. Katherine's stricken face roused an unaccustomed feeling in her breast, and she could not help but remember her promise to Henri. She had to remind herself that she was not breaking her promise by merely threatening the child.

"I see," said Katherine quietly. "What do you plan to do?"

Almost, Diantha relented, but she steeled herself with the thought of the ton, laughing at her. "What do you think I should do?" she asked. She did not wait for an answer. "I have debated the matter in my own mind and I must confess, I see no alternative but to go to Lord Ashington and tell him everything I know," she lied.

"I see," Katherine said again.

"Of course, if you were to promise me that you would leave London and never return, I might be willing to forget the whole matter," Diantha said. "I do want to be fair. 'Tis no one's business who you really are, so long as you don't try to pass yourself off as Quality."

Katherine was suddenly overwhelmed by a feeling of unutterable weariness. "I'll do it," she said. "I don't know quite how, but I will leave Freddy's house, as soon as is humanly possible."

Diantha rose. "You are very wise, my dear," she said. "It would be most unpleasant for you if you did not." As she looked down at Katherine, she realized that she had won, finally and irretrievably. Why, then, Diantha asked herself, did she feel so very miserable?

"YES, MY LORD, I SHALL marry you," Katherine said. Her face was very pale; she stood erect, back straight, only her clasping and unclasping hands showing her agitation. "I hope that you will never regret asking me. I promise you, I shall do all in my power to make you a good wife."

Katherine had spent all of the previous night in sleepless thought. She had tossed and turned, thinking about Lord Ashington. He did care for her, she was sure of it, but the more she thought about him, the more sure she became that she could never hope for happiness with him. Only two possibilities seemed likely to her: he would repudiate her when he learned of her background, or he would not, and be ruined by his magnanimity. Either would be too painful for her to bear, so, in the grey hours before dawn, she had at last decided that the best thing to do would be to wed Keswick. He had known of her past when he proposed to her; if he was willing to risk his position to marry her, at least he would be doing so with his eyes wide open. And she doubted that the ton would be as harsh towards Keswick as they would be towards Ashington. It was likely that they would shrug and chalk Keswick's *mésalliance* up to eccentricity. No such forbearance would be shown Ashington, she knew. He was too wealthy and too proud for his enemies not to rejoice in his lack of judgement.

"You have made me very happy, my love," Keswick said, eyeing his fiancé with concealed distaste. "I warn you, I plan on a hasty marriage. I simply cannot wait to have you all to myself." He turned to Freddy, an unhappy witness to their betrothal. "Come, Fred, will you not offer us felicitations?"

"Hope you'll be very happy," Freddy mumbled, looking down at the floor. He had been appalled when Katherine told him of Keswick's offer and of her plan to accept the peer. He had raged and threatened, cajoled and begged, but to no avail. Katherine was adamant and nothing he had said had swayed her. He had even gone so far as to appeal to Honoria.

"You can't let Kate marry that roué," he had told Honoria. "Put your foot down; forbid the match!"

Honoria had shaken her head, her expression glum. "It's the best thing," she had said. "She'll have no happiness longing for the moon. 'Tis better for her to wed Keswick than to remain unmarried and break her heart for what she cannot have." Honoria had suddenly looked very angry. "Love!" she had said. "Does it ever bring more happiness than pain? Poor Kate was cursed, cursed the very day she gave her heart to Ashington."

"Ashington!" Freddy had cried. "Do you mean to tell me that she's in love with Ashington?"

"Of course she is," Honoria had said. "Have you no eyes, boy? And the saddest thing of all is that I believe he cares for her, too."

"Then why can't she marry him?" Freddy had said in exasperation. "If they love each other..."

Honoria had looked at him sourly. "Do you really believe," she had asked, "that their love could survive the scandal?" Freddy had been unable to do more than gape at his aunt. "I suppose you thought that I didn't know," Honoria had said. "I'm not quite as great a fool as you imagine me to be, Freddy Basingstoke. Nothing goes on in this house that I don't know about." She shook her head. "I pity the child, truly I do. If Ashington loves her, he won't, or wouldn't if he found out, care if she came from a stable or from a palace. But others would; once the story got about, Ashington would be ruined. Think you that the ton would forgive Ashington the sin of marrying beneath him? You know better, and so does Kate. It would break the child's heart to be the instrument of Ashington's downfall. No, let her marry Keswick and try to find what happiness she can."

Freddy blinked, his mind full of his aunt's words, and found Keswick looking at him expectantly. "Beg your pardon?"

"I said, would you care to come to my club and celebrate with me?" Keswick said. "There are one or two things I should like to discuss with you."

"Very well," Freddy said reluctantly, and they bid Katherine farewell, Keswick bowing over her hand with languid grace. Not until they were out on the street did Keswick speak.

"You should congratulate yourself, Freddy," he said. "Not everyone can brag of having pulled the wool over the eyes of the Upper Ten Thousand, I do assure you."

Freddy's heart began to hammer in his chest. "What are you talking about?" he said.

"Oh, Kate told me her little secret," Keswick said. He looked at Freddy, who winced at the malice in his eyes. "I can understand why she wanted to fool us all, but I must confess, your part in the charade puzzles me. Why did you do it, Freddy? Why did you pass her off as blood?"

"Kate is related to me, albeit distantly," Freddy said.

"So it was loving kindness which made you do it? Try again, Basingstoke." Keswick's tone was cutting. "Or was it a matter of money, my friend? Did that harpy of a mother of hers pay you to present her to Society?" The shaft struck a little too close to home; Freddy's face must have reflected his thoughts. "I should have known," Keswick said.

"If you feel this way, why are you marrying her?" Freddy asked.

"But I have no choice, you see," Keswick said. "You've caught me, well and proper. I must marry Katherine, lest she tell her story to Ashington and he use it to ruin me."

"I don't understand," Freddy said. "How could it ruin *you?*"

"Katherine's late, sainted father was my cousin," Keswick said. "Do you see the humour in it, Freddy? I don't dare let this story get about, but the only way to stop it is to marry her myself." His voice was silky. "Lest you congratulate yourself too soon, though, pray be assured that Kate will pay for it, and in spades."

"You'll not marry her," Freddy said, meeting Keswick's gaze squarely. "Do you think I'd allow it, after hearing you speak of her in such a manner?"

"Oh, you'll allow it," Keswick said, with a pretence of amiability which chilled Freddy's soul. "You'll allow it, my friend, because you have no choice. If she cries off, I'll ruin her myself. Think you that I wouldn't do it? Be assured that I would."

"But *why?*" Freddy cried.

"Because, my dear Fred, if she doesn't accept me, I very much fear that Ashington will make her an offer. And we both know what she'll do, don't we? She'll tell him the story of her life. Ashington will know, and he will use the information to ruin me."

"How will he know that you are her cousin?" asked Freddy, trying hard to be reasonable.

Keswick shrugged delicately. "There was a certain amount of gossip, at the time, about that unfortunate carriage accident which killed Kate's mother's nurse. You may not recall it, but you may be sure that Ashington does. He was ever one to recall my sins! And it would give him great pleasure, I think, to drag the whole sordid story out for the ton to enjoy."

"He wouldn't do that," Freddy said stubbornly. "He cares for Kate; he wouldn't hurt her."

"Surely you can't believe I'd be content to rely on Ashington's kindness. No, my only recourse is to marry Kate." Keswick stared at Freddy, an ugly expression on his face. "If you truly care for the girl, Fred, you won't interfere with my plans. Otherwise, I shall destroy her."

CHAPTER TWELVE

FREDDY BASINGSTOKE swiped idly at a piece of greenery with his cane, his brow furrowed in a frown. He was standing in front of Lord Ashington's London residence and had been for some time, worrying and wondering what he should do. For a day and a night Freddy had brooded about Keswick and Katherine; for a day and a night he had fretted about whether or not he should tell Ashington what was afoot. On the one hand, Freddy took Keswick's threats to ruin Katherine very seriously. He knew that the peer was ruthless enough to go to any lengths to achieve his purpose. On the other hand, he could not bear the thought of Katherine giving herself to such a one, particularly as he was quite sure that Keswick would make her life a living hell. Freddy suspected that the only way to stop the marriage was to tell Ashington of Keswick's plans for Katherine. And that, he thought, was the crux of the matter. Could he make Ashington understand the danger to Katherine, without betraying Katherine's secret?

''Fred?''

Freddy's head jerked up and he whirled round. Ashington was seated on the front steps of his house, smiling at his friend, for all the world as if it were the most normal thing imaginable for a peer of the realm to repose himself on a stairway.

"Ash!" Freddy stammered. "Good—good morning."

"I've been sitting up in my dining room watching you pace back and forth for the last twenty minutes," Ashington said. "Have you decided yet?"

"Decided what?" Freddy asked.

"Whether or not you're going to tell me about whatever it is that's troubling you?" Ashington said calmly. "Much better to, I think; I can't help you unless I know what's wrong."

"Oh, Ash," Freddy said miserably. "I've made such a mess of it!"

"Come inside and we'll see what we may do to set things right," Ashington said. "Not that I have the faintest notion of what you're talking about. But it must be something fairly awful to send you into such a funk."

Ashington and Freddy went inside. Ashington waved his butler away, and the pair made themselves comfortable in the study, the brandy decanter close at hand.

"Well, Fred?" asked Ashington. "What's amiss?"

"Ash, do you care for Kate?" Freddy asked abruptly.

Ashington choked a little on his brandy. "Of course I do," he said. "You did ask me to stand as foster brother to her, did you not?"

"I mean, more than that," Freddy said. "Romantically."

"Zounds, Fred, but you do ask some questions!" Ashington protested. "May one enquire what your interest in the matter is?"

Freddy shifted uncomfortably in his seat. "I am somewhat of a guardian to her, you know," he said. "'Tis not outrageous that I should ask you such a question."

Ashington avoided answering. "It couldn't be that which has made you look so troubled," he said. "You must know that I would never do anything to hurt Kate?"

"Of course I do," Freddy said impatiently. "But I need to know... Do you care for her?" He met Ashington's gaze. "Do you?"

It was Ashington's turn to look uncomfortable. "Damn you, Freddy, for making me feel such a fool! Yes." Ashington let out his breath with a feeling of relief. "Yes, I do care for her; I have only lately begun to realize how much. Does that satisfy you?"

If anything, Freddy looked even more miserable. "Do you wish to wed her?" he blurted out.

Ashington's brows snapped together in a frown. "Now, that is quite enough," he said. "I've answered your questions very patiently, I think, but now you've gone a little beyond the line. Why are you asking me these things? What is it?"

Freddy rose to his feet and took an agitated turn about the room. "It's so hard to know what's best to do," he confessed. "It's all such a muddle."

Ashington was beginning to feel the first, faint stirrings of alarm. "Tell me, Fred," he demanded, "is it Kate? Is she ill?"

"No, no, not ill," Freddy said, then went on disjointedly, "he said such things to me, Ash...about how he would treat her, and how he would make her pay!"

Ashington gave an exasperated sigh. "Freddy," he said, "you're raving. Lest you wish me to end up in Bedlam—no doubt in the same cell as yourself—you must tell me what is troubling you."

"It's Kate," Freddy said.

"Yes, yes, but *what* about her?" Ashington snapped. "Now, Freddy!"

"And Keswick," Freddy went on, as though he had not heard Ashington. "They're...that is to say...well..." He looked up at his friend unhappily. "They're betrothed."

Ashington stared at Freddy for a moment, then, much to Freddy's amazement, smiled. "No," he said gently. "You must be mistaken."

"I promise you, Ash, I—"

"Did you quarrel with Kate? She must have told you that just to annoy you. It was wrong of her, I know, but you mustn't take it to heart," Ashington said.

"I'm not wrong, Ash," Freddy said heavily. "I was there when she accepted his offer."

"But she couldn't have... She wouldn't..." Ashington could feel the blood beginning to pound in his head and the colour coursing up into his face.

"She could," Freddy answered. "She did. And I hope, so long as I live, never to see such unhappiness in anyone's face as I saw in hers when she said yes," Freddy said.

"She will not marry him," Ashington said flatly. He turned and shouted for his butler.

"But how can we stop her, Ash?" Freddy asked. "I've gone over it again and again in my mind, but if Katherine is determined to wed Keswick, how can we stop her?"

"Very easily, my friend." In a voice which made Freddy shudder, Ashington gave his butler instructions to call for his curricle, then turned back to his friend. "Whatever happens, Katherine Crest will not marry Lord Keswick," he said. "For however devoted she may be to him, she may not marry a corpse, and that, my dear Fred, is what Keswick will be, before this day has passed!"

LORD KESWICK CLOSED the door slowly behind his visitor. His normal aplomb had deserted him; he crossed shakily to the sideboard and poured himself a stiff brandy, then another, before he sank back down behind his desk.

His mouth twisted in a grimace. Who would ever have thought that he would have cause to be grateful for his failure to engage a new butler? Had he had one, he would not have opened the door himself; had he not opened the door himself, his caller might never have managed to see him, and Keswick would never have known in what danger he stood. He raised the glass to his lips and noticed that his hands were shaking. Telling himself not to succumb to panic, he sat back to review what he had learned.

His caller had been a small, brown Frenchman named Forcat, Maître Etienne Forcat. He had all but forced his way into Keswick's study. First annoyed, then amused by the little man's tenacity, Keswick had let him in, then invited him to state his business.

Maître Forcat was a solicitor, he had informed Keswick. His specialty was tracking down the lost and missing, and he had the deep honour, he had said, to be employed by His Royal Highness, King Louis XVIII of France.

"Most enthralling, I'm sure," Keswick had replied, "but I fail to see what has brought you to me. I am not missing, nor, to the best of my knowledge, have I ever been lost."

"Oh, no, *monseigneur,* it is not you that I seek, but your young relative," Maître Forcat had said earnestly.

Keswick had felt the first faint stirrings of alarm. "What young relative?" he had asked. "I am the last surviving member of my family. Sadly, I have no relatives, young or otherwise."

"*Mais non, monseigneur,* I believe that you do," Forcat had insisted. "Have you not a cousin, by the name of—" he had consulted a paper "—Henry Keswick?"

Keswick had shrugged. "What of it? He has been dead for many years."

"Yes, but before he died, he married a young French lady named L'Ecusson," Forcat had said. "Marie L'Ecusson."

Keswick had felt the cold sweat on his forehead, but had managed to keep his face impassive. "You are mistaken, monsieur," he had told the solicitor. "My cousin died unwed."

"I believe not," Maître Forcat had said, polite but puzzled by Keswick's adamance. "The young lady wrote a letter to her father, informing him of her marriage and of the subsequent birth of a son. I have the letter right here." He had patted his pocket.

"Oh, well!" Keswick had feigned unconcern. "Any whore—" he had said the word deliberately and watched the Frenchman flinch "—any whore could write such a letter to excuse her own sin. That does not make it true. I assure you, my cousin could not have married without my family learning of it."

"Then you have no information which might help me to find the family?" The Frenchman was still polite, but his brown eyes had looked coldly into Keswick's own.

"None whatsoever," Keswick had said. "So, monsieur, I should suggest that you abandon this futile mission. In fact, I insist upon it." Keswick had leaned forward threateningly. "I am not without a certain power in this country. I should be most unhappy with you, Monsieur Forcat, if you should embarrass me by pursuing these enquiries."

The man had had the effrontery to smile. "I shall persist," he had replied. "Your government has been kind enough to promise me every assistance in this matter. A favour to His Majesty King Louis, I believe." He had risen to his feet. "In fact, they have already been most helpful to me, most helpful indeed. They assisted me in locating the inn at which my young lady resided when her last letters were received in France. Fortunately, the concierge at the inn remembered Marie clearly, and the name of the young gentleman that Marie had wed—Henry Keswick, to be precise. She thought the story *très romantique.*" Maître Forcat had smiled blandly at Keswick. "That is what led me to you, *monseigneur.* Are you quite sure...?"

"Quite!"

"I thank you for your time, then, *monseigneur,* and your help."

"I've given you no help!" Keswick had snarled.

"Ah, but you have, my Lord Keswick," the man had said. He had bowed and turned towards the door.

"Forcat!" The solicitor had halted on the doorstep. "Why are you so anxious to find this young whelp?" The question had been torn from Keswick.

"Ah, *monseigneur*," the Frenchman had said. "As you English say, that would be telling!" With that, he had left.

Keswick ran a hand over his forehead and considered his options. Whatever reasons the French solicitor had for seeking Henri L'Ecusson could bode no good for Keswick. Should the man continue his search, the truth would be bound to come out and Keswick would be ruined. No one knew that Katherine was Henri's sister, but Keswick knew from firsthand experience that the girl could not be relied upon to keep her mouth closed.

Keswick finished his brandy and rose purposefully to his feet. There was no help for it, then; he must elope with Katherine, and that very day. Once he had wed the girl, he could bury her at one of his homes in the country. She'd tell no one her story, because there would be no one there to tell.

Keswick wasted no time. He informed his valet that he would be away from Town for several days and had the man pack a bag for him. Then he sent for his coach and set out.

AT FREDDY'S, KATHERINE sat alone in the drawing-room. She had been there all morning; she did not notice the passage of time, or know how long she had been sitting there when Croaker entered the room. "A caller, miss," he said, then noticed her pallor and the curious way she was sitting, as though something in her were broken. "Are you well, Miss Kate?" he asked anxiously.

"What? I'm fine, Croaker. Who is it?"

"My lord Keswick, miss. Shall I send him away?"

"Too late, I fear," came Keswick's languid tones. "I took the liberty of showing myself in, Kate. I knew you wouldn't mind." His eyes narrowed as he spied his betrothed. "That will be all, Croaker," he said.

The butler stiffened in outrage, but permitted himself only a sniff of disapproval before leaving the room.

"What is it, my dear?" Keswick asked. "What's wrong?"

"It's Diantha," Katherine said. "She knows."

"How did she find out?" Keswick asked sharply. "Damn you, Kate, tell me!"

Katherine did not seem to notice his harsh words. "I don't know," she said, and raised blank eyes to Keswick. "She said . . . she said she'd tell Ashington, if I didn't leave London forever."

Keswick's tight shoulders relaxed. "Well, then," he said, "we shall do it."

"Do what?"

"We shall leave London, today," Keswick said.

"But how can we do that?" Katherine asked. She pressed her hands hard against her eyes. "I can't think," she said.

"Then simply listen," Keswick told her. "We'll leave Town this very instant and go to Gretna Green. We can be married there." Katherine did not answer. "Are you listening, Kate?" he said. "We'll elope."

"Elope?" Katherine looked dazed. "We can't do that...you don't want to do that, my lord. Do you?" He heard the dawning hope in her voice.

"Yes," he said. "I do, very much." As he took her hand, Keswick reflected grimly that he would not have to keep up this charade for very much longer. "There's nothing I want more than to be married to you," he said. "This accords perfectly with my wishes, I do assure you."

"Are you...are you sure, my lord?" Katherine asked. She saw that it was the only solution; to leave London, Lady Blandford and Lord Ashington behind her and to start her new life with Keswick.

He pulled her to her feet. "Quite sure," he said. "You may believe me when I say, Kate, that there is nothing on Earth that I desire quite so much."

FREDDY ALL BUT HOPPED back and forth from foot to foot, so impatient was he. As soon as her maid opened the door to Kate's room, he said, "Well? Is she within?"

"No, sir," the maid said.

"Damn!" said Freddy Basingstoke. He loped down the stairs.

"She's not in her room, either," he told Ashington, who was waiting in the foyer. "The maid ain't seen her for hours."

"What about Aunt Honoria?" Ashington asked.

"Honoria's been gone all day; went to visit some crony of hers in Bath," Freddy said gloomily. He turned to Croaker, the butler. "And you say the last time you saw her was when Lord Keswick called?"

The butler nodded. "If I may be so bold, sir, my lord, Miss Kate seemed somewhat...distracted this morning."

"Distracted?" Ashington said sharply.

"It appeared," said Croaker, staring off into space, "that Miss Kate had been napping her bib—that is to say, weeping," he corrected himself hastily.

At that moment, the knocker on the front door sounded. Croaker looked at Freddy; with a jerk of his head, Freddy motioned to the man to open the door. "Whoever it is, tell them we're not at home."

Diantha, Countess of Blandford, swept imperiously into the house, her maid close behind. "I wish to see Miss Crest," she said before Croaker could speak. She started when she caught sight of Freddy and Ashington.

"Ash! I...good morning," she said in confusion.

Ashington looked at her through narrowed eyes; his frown deepened. "What are you doing here?" he said without preamble.

Diantha raised her head proudly. "I'm sure I don't need to account for my actions to you, Ashington," she said coldly. "I've come to see Miss Crest. Would you please be so good, Freddy, as to inform her that I am here?"

"He can't," Ashington said. "She's gone."

Diantha almost groaned aloud. She had given up trying to convince herself that she had done what she ought when she went to Katherine with her threats. She was filled with an unaccustomed sense of shame; the fear that Henri would learn of her actions and despise her forever did not improve her state of mind. Diantha could not quite work out why it was that Henri's opinion was so important to her, but she knew that at this particular moment, she would much rather have Henri's approbation than, say, Ashington's. So she had come to Freddy's to try to set things right.

Ashington watched Diantha's face closely, then added, "Just as I thought. What mischief have you been up to, Diantha?"

"I'm sure I don't know what you mean," Diantha said, her face pale. "If Miss Crest is not at home, pray tell her that I shall call again later." The countess turned towards the door.

"Oh, no," said Ashington grimly, grabbing Diantha's wrist. "You'll tell me what you've done, Diantha, and you'll do so now!"

Freddy became aware that Croaker and Dorcas, Diantha's maid, were watching the scene with great interest. "Perhaps we should step into the morning room," he said hastily. "A private matter, don't you know."

The three filed into the morning room and Freddy shut the door firmly.

"Now, Di, out with it," Ashington said. "Where is she?"

Diantha tried once more to brazen her way through. "I can't imagine what you are going on about," she said.

"Don't lie to me, Diantha!" Ashington snapped.

Diantha opened her mouth to lie, then looked at Ashington and thought better of it. "I came here to call on Katherine earlier," she began weakly.

"And?"

"And I told her...I told her..." Diantha could feel Freddy's eyes upon her, willing her not to tell Ashington Katherine's secret. "I told her," she whispered, "that if she did not leave London, then I would tell you, Ashington..." She stopped.

"Tell me what? Good Lord, Di, what could you possibly have to tell me about Kate?" Ashington's temper was fast slipping out of his control.

"I was very bad," Diantha said weakly. "I knew that you loved her, and that she loved you. But I could not accept it; I was jealous and angry, Ash. Please try to understand!"

Ashington took a step towards Diantha. "What have you done?" he asked, in a dangerously quiet voice.

"I—I told Katherine that I would tell you a pack of lies about her lack of virtue. I told her that she would be ruined, and that you would never have anything to do with her again." She met Ashington's eyes, her own filled with tears. "I'm sorry!" she cried. "I was wrong. I knew that you were through with me, Ash. But I was so very, very angry!" Her shoulders slumped. "I never meant to hurt her, I swear."

"You didn't mean to hurt her?" Ashington repeated angrily. "Then exactly what did you mean, Diantha? I could cheerfully... Never mind!"

"That's not important now," Diantha said. "We know now why Katherine went. The question is, where did she go? Where could she have gone?" She wrung her hands. "I'll never forgive myself if anything has happened to her!"

Freddy was thinking hard. "If Keswick has been here," he said slowly, "it's possible that they may have eloped. Keswick is quite determined to have her; he knows—" his voice dropped "—that you love her, Ash."

"Of course," Diantha said. "Of course that's what they've done! Why didn't I realize it?"

"This makes no sense," Ashington said. "Why would Kate think that I'd believe Diantha's lies? Has she no more faith in me than that?"

"We have no time for this," Freddy broke in. "They've eloped and we've got to stop them. Let's go!"

"Let me come with you," Diantha pleaded. "Let me help."

"I believe," said Ashington crushingly, "that you've helped quite enough already." With that, Freddy and Ashington were gone.

Diantha stood alone in the morning room for a long moment, her shoulders drooping. Then she opened the door and called for her maid. "Dorcas," she said, pulling on her gloves, "are you familiar with a tailor shop called L'Ecusson?"

CHAPTER THIRTEEN

KATHERINE NERVOUSLY twisted the strings of her reticule. She had stopped for nothing on her flight from Freddy's; Keswick had convinced her that they could buy what they needed on the road and that to pack even a bandbox would be to risk being discovered before they could make good their escape. Keswick, perfectly at ease, leaned his head back against the velvet squabs of the coach, eyes closed. For the first time Katherine noticed the deep lines which cut from his nose to the corners of his mouth, and the faint scorn in his expression, even in repose. She realized that she barely knew this man whom she was about to marry. Did he really love her so deeply that he was willing to throw convention to the wind and marry her out of hand? Despite herself, she could not help but feel that there was more to Keswick's eagerness to elope with her than mere passion.

Keswick opened his eyes and looked across the coach, unblinking, at his soon-to-be-bride. "Well, my dear?" he asked. "Shall I do?"

"I'm—I'm sorry, my lord," Katherine said and smiled shyly. "I did not mean to stare."

"Not at all," said Keswick with equanimity. "'Tis perfectly natural that you be curious about your husband—will he treat you well? Will he be kind?"

"I'm sure I need have no such fears with you, my lord," Katherine said. "You have been all that is most kind to me."

"Indeed," said Keswick. "I have been thinking about where to take you after we are wed. Keswick Hall will do nicely, I think."

"Is it near here, my lord?"

"Do you know, Kate, I think it might be more comfortable if you were to call me Keswick," her fiancé said. "It is just a little tiresome to hear 'my lord' this and 'my lord' that."

"I'm sorry, my...Keswick," said Katherine.

"As to your question, no, Keswick Hall is not near here, particularly," he said. "'Tis in the wilds of Lancashire, as a matter of fact."

"So far from London?" asked Katherine in surprise. "Will you not miss your Town life?"

Keswick raised one eyebrow. "You cannot think that I shall stay there with you?" he asked. "No, no, my dear, that would not suit me at all, I'm afraid."

The coach was silent for a moment, then Katherine said hesitantly, "I suppose it would discourage talk if you returned to Town right away. Will you...will you want me to join you in London?"

"Not at all, my dear," Keswick said.

Katherine breathed a sigh of relief. "I must admit, my...Keswick, I would be happier in the country."

Where you won't need to see Ashington! a voice inside of her jeered.

"No," continued Keswick, "I feel no special need to have a wife in Town, interfering with my pleasures. My life will go along very nicely without you." Katherine's expression was eloquent; Keswick added, "That is not to say that you will not see me from time to time, often enough for me to keep you with child, at any rate." He looked her up and down. "It shouldn't be too unpleasant a task," he remarked.

Katherine stared at Keswick. Her heart was beating so hard that she could barely hear the sound of her own voice. "What are you saying, my lord?" she asked. "I don't understand."

"Surely you didn't believe that I would bring you back to Town and take the chance that your sordid little secret would become known?" Keswick shook his head. "No, my dear, you will stay at Keswick Hall, where you will have the time and leisure to contemplate your sins."

"What sins?" Katherine asked quietly.

Keswick suddenly seemed furiously angry. "The sin of pride," he snarled. "The sin that made you—you, a shopgirl!—believe that you were good enough to marry a peer of the realm. I could laugh, were I not so sickened, at how neatly you trapped me, my dear. How the mighty have fallen! But I shall not be the only one to suffer, sweet Kate, I promise you that."

Katherine was stunned by the hatred she saw in Keswick's eyes. "Why are you marrying me?" she whispered. "Why are we here?"

"You still don't understand, do you? You are more like your father than I had imagined. Henry, too, was ever the fool, living in a world of illusion."

"You knew my father?"

Keswick laughed bitterly. "He was my cousin," he said. "Though he rued that fact almost as much as I did; we hated each other, you see. This troubled poor, foolish Henry a great deal. He felt ashamed that he should so cordially dislike one so young and so closely related to him. That is why he let me drive his curricle that day, I think; to try to still the pangs of conscience and to make a friend of me. It almost worked. I almost had him convinced that I was not half so black as he had painted me, until that cursed woman stepped out in front of us."

Katherine drew in her breath in horror. "It was *you?*"

"It was her own fault. She should have watched where she was going," Keswick said, with a coldheartedness which made Katherine shudder. "And the effrontery of that French chit, your mother! She dared to call me a murderer. Your father supported her, of course; no such thing as family loyalty for our Henry. I had the last laugh, though, when he came to present his bride to my uncle and the old man threw him out, bag and baggage." Keswick turned icy blue eyes on Katherine. "Then you came along, my dear, and trapped me, as neatly as the veriest courtesan—my own dear cousin, reeking with the stench of the shop. I must marry you, unfortunately. Can you imagine the joy it would give the tattlemongers of the ton, to point at me and whisper? My reputation could not withstand such a blow." He smiled, a smile which made Katherine shudder anew. "I will have one more little bit of pleasure out of all this, though. I am quite looking forward to telling your mother what all her scheming has come to. Do you see the delicious irony of it all? Her plans and all her plotting have brought you to marriage with the one man she hates above all others on Earth."

"No," Katherine said.

"No what?"

"There will be no marriage, my lord," Katherine said. "Can you think that I would wed you now, knowing who and what you are? You must be mad."

Keswick's hand shot forward. He grabbed Katherine's wrist and squeezed until she cried out. "Start as you mean to go on, my dear," he said in a deceptively gentle voice. "You will marry me. You will obey me, in every particular, or you will be very, very sorry."

Katherine grimaced with pain, but held her ground. "You cannot make me say 'I do,'" she said. "You cannot force me...."

"I can," he contradicted her. "Do you cross me, I will go straight back to London and destroy your family. 'Twill not take more than a word or two, spoken in the right ear. Perhaps a suggestion that your brother was a spy during our late war with France? Or I might say that I went to order a coat and your mother stole my purse. Would you like to see your family transported?''

"No one would believe you!" Katherine cried.

"Ah, but they would," Keswick said evenly; only the glitter in his eyes betrayed his enjoyment. "I am a peer, don't forget, and a member of the House of Lords. You cannot think that the authorities would take the word of a tailor over mine?''

Katherine sat in broken silence. Keswick was right, she knew. If he were to make any accusation, however absurd, against Henri and Marie, it would be believed. The choice was simple: her own happiness, or the happiness and well-being of her family.

Keswick read her answer in her eyes. "I thought you'd see it my way," he said, and leaned his head back again, his lips curled in a satisfied smile.

ASHINGTON CLIMBED BACK into the curricle and whipped up the horses. "The ostler said they passed through about half an hour ago," he told Freddy. "We should catch up with them soon; I daresay they'll be stopping shortly, if only to change horses again." Dusk was just falling; Freddy and Ashington had been on the road for several hours and had made excellent time, thanks to the superb quality of Ashington's horses.

Freddy yawned and stretched his legs out as best he could in the cramped quarters of the curricle. "It can't be soon enough for me," he said. "Lord, I don't remember when last I was so bumped and shaken."

"I, too, am passing anxious to find them," Ashington said. "Or, more precisely, to find Keswick."

Freddy's head swivelled round. "You aren't really going to kill him, are you, Ash? You can't do that," Freddy said. "You know you can't!"

"I may have to," Ashington said quietly. "How else am I to get Kate away from him? I can't very well say, 'Sorry, old boy, but I'm here to kidnap your fiancée. You don't mind, do you?' Dash it all, Fred, Kate did go with him of her own free will."

"By now, she's sorry she's gone," Freddy said. "She'll be glad to see us, I'm sure of it."

"How can you be so sure?"

"Because she loves you," Freddy said. "She was afraid, and confused; she didn't want you to find out..." he stopped.

"Find out what?" Ashington asked. "Damn your eyes, Fred, I wish you'd tell me what's going on!"

Freddy shook his head. "I can't," he said. "It's not my tale to tell." He slid a sidelong look at his friend. "How did you know that she was keeping something from you?" he asked.

Ashington shrugged. "Kate has no gift for subterfuge," he said. "She told me that she had just come to England, but you said that she had been here for some time, at school. Honoria all but told me she was very well to do, but Kate told me that she was poor, relatively speaking. And why would Kate think I'd believe anything Diantha might say about her? I would have had to be awfully dense not to suspect that there was something amiss." He frowned. "But mainly, it was Kate herself," he said. "She cares for me, I know she does, but she seems...almost afraid, if that makes sense. It tears at my heart to see her so unhappy." He looked at Freddy. "But I tell you now, Fred, I'll have no secrets between us. I love Kate and I want to marry her, but not until she tells me whatever it is that she's tried so hard to keep from me."

"She will tell you," Freddy said with great certainty. "I know she will." *And pray God,* he thought to himself, *that you will still love her when you know!*

THE BELL ON THE BACK of the shop door tinkled. Marie L'Ecusson turned to greet her customer, then said with a smile, "I'm sorry, miss, but I believe you have the wrong shop. Perhaps you are seeking the dressmaker, two doors down?"

The woman shook her head and pulled the hood of her shabby cloak a little closer about her face. "No," she said in a gruff voice. "This is where I mean to be. Is Henri in?"

"He is abovestairs," Marie said. "May I help you?"

"No!" the woman said. "I must see Henri. Please call him down."

"*Pardon,* mademoiselle, but I am mistress here," Marie said. "You do not give orders in my shop."

"But I must see him," the woman said, a note of desperation in her voice. "It's urgent...a matter of gravest import!"

Marie frowned and looked more closely at her visitor. The hand which held the hood tightly about the woman's face was soft and unblemished, and though her clothes were of the cheapest sort, Marie judged that the woman's shoes were custom-made, and of the finest Italian leather.

"Come, *chérie,*" Marie said more kindly. "Tell me what is so urgent that you must see my son. And take your hood down; there is no need to be frightened here."

Slowly the woman pulled the hood down around her shoulders. Marie almost laughed aloud, but managed to control herself. The woman's hair was pitch black, or rather, Marie thought, lampblack, a colour obviously not her own. The black had rubbed off on her forehead and cheeks. Rouge had been rubbed into her cheeks to disguise the fair white complexion beneath; the effect was not altogether salubrious. The woman looked at Marie pleadingly. "Please send for Henri," she said. "I must speak to him."

"I'm sorry," Marie said, "but until I know what all this is about—"

The woman stamped her foot. "Send for him, I said, and now!" she snapped.

Marie's eyebrows soared. In her anger, the woman had forgotten to use her gruff voice; her natural tone showed her to be of gentle birth. Marie looked at her visitor for another long moment, then bowed her head. "Very well, mademoiselle," she said quietly. She crossed to the foot of the stairs and called up, "Henri! Henri, come down, please. I have need of you."

A moment later, Henri L'Ecusson ran lightly down the stairs. "What is it, Maman?" he said. "I was just..." He rocked to a halt. "Diantha!" he cried. "What are you doing here?"

Diantha, Countess of Blandford, flew across the room to Henri. "Henri, thank God," she said, half sobbing. "There's not a moment to lose!"

"Softly, *ma chérie,* softly," Henri said, taking Diantha by the elbow and steering her to a nearby chair. "What has upset you so? And why the disguise?" The hint of a smile in his eyes, Henri touched Diantha's hair with one finger. "Lampblack, *n'est ce pas?*"

"Yes, yes, but that's not important," Diantha said. "Henri, Kate is in the gravest danger."

Marie took a step forward. "Kate?" she said sharply. "What is wrong with my daughter?"

Diantha turned to Marie, her mind distracted for a moment. "You are Henri's mama?" she said, aghast. "Madame, I am so very sorry if I was rude, but..."

"Yes, yes, but what is wrong with Kate?" Marie cried.

"Oh, Henri, she's eloped," Diantha said miserably. "And it's all my fault. She never would have gone with him if I hadn't been so cruel."

"Eloped?" Henri repeated blankly.

Marie gave a sigh of relief. "Is that all?" she said. "Oh, it is true, an elopement is not what I should have chosen for my dear Katherine, but if the gentleman loves her so that he must run off with her, well, it bodes well for her happiness, does it not?"

"No, no, you don't understand," Diantha said impatiently. "He doesn't love her! In fact, I do believe that he despises her."

"But why should he marry her, then?" Henri was puzzled.

Diantha gave a bitter laugh. "Who can know why my lord Keswick does anything?" she said.

Marie L'Ecusson gasped and pressed her hand to her heart. "Keswick?" she said, her face as white as paper. "Lord Arthur Keswick?" Diantha nodded.

Marie groaned and crumpled in a faint. Henri darted across the room and caught his mother before she hit the floor. "Maman! What is it?"

"Bring her here, Henri," Diantha said, rising to her feet. She helped Henri settle his mother in the chair and loosen her clothing. Digging through her reticule, Diantha brought out a bottle of smelling salts and waved the bottle under the Frenchwoman's nose.

Marie coughed; her eyelids fluttered, then opened. "Henri," she whispered. "You must stop this marriage. Katherine must not be allowed to marry that spawn of hell!"

"But, Maman," Henri protested. "If she loves him..."

"She doesn't love Keswick," Diantha said. "She just went with him because... because..." Diantha's voice quavered. "I have been very wicked, Henri."

Marie caught Henri's wrist in her hand. "Do you not see, my son? It was Keswick who killed my Hélène, Keswick who turned your father's family against us. He is an evil man, the most evil that I have ever known. Stop them, Henri. Stop him!"

"I shall, Maman," Henri said grimly. "Diantha, pray take my mother abovestairs and settle her in her bed. I am off to order a coach and four; I shall return before I set out after them."

Diantha met Henri's gaze squarely. "I am going with you," she said.

"Diantha, there is no time," Henri began.

"I am going with you," Diantha said again. "If you don't take me with you, I shall call for my carriage and follow you." She caught Henri's hand in both her own. "Please, Henri, please," she said tearfully. "'Tis all my fault. I must do what I can to set things right!"

Henri was torn. "But what about Maman?" he said. "I was going to ask you to stay with her, until I return."

"Never you fear, Henri," Marie said, her voice already stronger. "The best medicine in the world for me is the knowledge that you will stop this marriage. I shall be fine. Now go!"

KATHERINE HUDDLED AT ONE end of the dining table, her food untouched before her. She drooped with weariness; she and Keswick had travelled hard that day, not stopping until almost half their journey had been accomplished, and then only to change horses. She had not spoken to the groom, who had hitched up the fresh horses, nor to the serving man who had brought their dinner at the second stop. Each time, Keswick had gripped her arm tight and whispered to her, "No trouble, now, my dear. Remember your family!"

Lord Keswick was sprawled in an armchair before the fire, a bottle of brandy near at hand. He watched her with some amusement. "Ashington would not think you so pretty," he remarked, "if he could see you now. You do not travel well, my sweet."

Katherine did not bother to answer him; she was too lost in a fog of misery and anguish to be hurt by his unkind comments. How could she have been so very foolish? she asked herself. She should have seen what kind of creature Keswick was. She should have listened to Freddy and Ashington and kept her distance from the man who would now force her to wed him. Most of all she regretted not telling Ashington the truth. He might have despised her for it, but no more than he would for marrying his enemy.

"Still brooding about Ashington, I see," Keswick said perceptively. "It will do you no good, my dear. Whatever his faults, Ashington would never trifle with a married lady. Besides which, I think it highly unlikely that you will ever set eyes on him again."

"I should not be so sure of that if I were you," Lord Ashington said; he had opened the door to the private parlour so quietly that neither Keswick nor Katherine had heard it.

"Ash!" Katherine cried. Her face alight with joy, she leapt to her feet. "Thank God you've come."

As Ashington's eyes met Katherine's across the room, all doubts were banished from Ashington's mind. He swiftly crossed the room to her side, and took her hands in his own. "Are you all right, Kate?" he asked. "Has he hurt you?" He smiled down at her and smoothed the tangled black hair from her brow.

"No, no," Katherine said, and began to quietly cry. "But, oh, Ash, I have been so very foolish."

"There, now, pet, don't cry," he said tenderly, and put his arms round her. "You can't know what an effect it has on me."

Katherine smiled through her tears and snuggled happily in his embrace.

"This is all very touching, I'm sure," Keswick said. "But I would be most appreciative, Ashington, if you would unhand my fiancée."

Ashington did not even look at Keswick. "Your engagement is at an end," he said. "Kate can't marry us both, and I do think that she prefers me to you. Don't you, love?"

"I think not," said Keswick. He turned a frigid blue gaze on Katherine. "Do tell him, Kate, and remember... your family depends on you."

Katherine lifted her chin. "I shall never marry you," she said. "Ashington would not let you hurt my family."

"No?" Keswick sneered. "Even when he learns that you are no better than a tailor's get? I should very much like to see our proud Lord Ashington explain to the ton why he has chosen to marry a shopgirl."

Freddy had stood silently at the back of the room until this point, but now he stepped forward. "That's enough, Keswick," he said. "Another word and I vow, I'll plant you a facer!"

Keswick lifted his quizzing glass and surveyed Freddy insultingly. "Will you really, Freddy?" he asked. "I hardly think it worthwhile for you to bother defending a lady—a *person,* that is to say—of Kate's—" That was enough for Frederick Basingstoke, Esquire. He drew back his fist and, with all the strength of his lanky body, dealt Keswick a blow which knocked him to the floor. Freddy stared at his own fist in awe. "I don't believe it," he said. "All those boxing lessons from Gentleman Jack and he swore I'd not learned anything. I guess this proves him wrong, doesn't it, Ash?"

But Ashington did not answer him. He had not said a word since Keswick had told him Katherine's secret. Kate had felt his body stiffen at his words, and now she tried to explain. "Ash," she began. "My French grandfather was a *comte*..." Quickly she told him the story Marie had shared with her, of her father's birth and disinheritance, of Marie's family's destruction in the French Revolution and her discovery that Keswick was her cousin. She told Ash how she had tried to get Keswick to return her to London, and of his threats against her family. At the end, she stared pleadingly up at the tall man. "You do understand, don't you, Ash?" she said. "Don't you?"

"Why didn't you tell me?" he asked, staring down into her eyes, his face unreadable. "You should have told me." He turned towards the window.

"This is all most interesting, but it is time that Katherine and I continued our journey," Lord Keswick said. He held one hand to his bruised face; the other held a small pistol, the barrel fixed steadily on Katherine. "You look surprised, my dear. Did you think that Freddy had disposed of me so easily? You should know better than that—ever the bad penny, you see." He jerked the barrel of the gun, motioning Katherine away from Freddy and Ashington. "I've set you a tantalizing puzzle, have I not, my lord?" he asked Ashington. "You have the weapon of my destruction in your hand, yet you dare not use it. After all, how can you ruin me without also ruining Kate? My wife would be bound to suffer as I did; even more, for I promise you that I should spend my life tormenting her, should I have no social outlets to distract my mind."

"The question will not arise," Ashington said. "Whatever happens, you will not marry Kate." A carriage could be heard pulling into the courtyard outside, but no one in the room looked away from Keswick.

"Oh, but I shall," Keswick said. He grabbed Katherine's arm. "She is doubly important to me now; she will serve to ensure your silence." He began to pull her back towards the door. "Pray do not attempt to follow us, gentlemen. I am quite determined that little Kate shall wed me. So determined, in fact, that were I to be thwarted, I might be forced to do something drastic."

The parlour door opened and Lady Honoria Basingstoke marched into the room. "Here you are," she said accusingly. "My dear girl, I've been all over Creation searching for you." She looked round the room. "I hardly thought, when I set out after you, Kate, that I would be part of a caravan. Between Freddy, Ashington, myself and the pair I met on the road, I should think that this must be the largest elopement in history!" Honoria spared a disapproving glare for Keswick. "Good Lord, Keswick, do stop play-acting," she snapped.

Lord Keswick was startled. As he looked at Honoria, the barrel of his gun wavered. This was all the opportunity that Ashington needed; he leapt across the room and, with one well-placed blow, finished the job Freddy had started.

Henri burst into the parlour shouting, "Kate!" Katherine hurried to her brother's side. "Thank God, *ma chére,*" he said, and threw his arms round her. "I was so worried—when we learned what had hap-

pened, and Maman told me who this Keswick was . . .
Thank God you're all right," he said again.

Diantha swayed into the room, for all the world as
though she were entering a London ballroom; she had
obviously quite forgotten the lampblack that covered
her hair and, by now, most of her face also. "Kate!"
She hurried to the girl's side, both hands outstretched. "I was certain we'd find you."

Katherine blanched, but held her ground. "You are
too late, my lady," she said bitterly. "Ashington already knows."

Diantha blushed and hung her head. "Diantha?"
prompted Henri gently.

"I am very sorry," Diantha said. Katherine was
surprised to see that her green eyes were filled with
tears. "I have been very, very wicked, and I do beg
your pardon, Miss . . . Kate."

"An apology does not begin to excuse your sins,
Diantha," Ashington said acerbically. "We shall
speak of it later."

"No, my lord, you will not," said Henri. He met the
peer's gaze squarely. "Diantha has asked pardon very
prettily, and I think that Kate will be inclined to grant
it, once she hears our news."

Katherine looked back and forth between Henri and
Diantha, her brow furrowed. "What news?" she
asked.

Henri took Diantha's hand. "I am the luckiest of
men," he said. "Diantha has agreed to be my bride."

Katherine's mouth fell open; Henri stepped closer to his sister and said, for her ears only, "I know that you are surprised, *ma soeur.* Perhaps you think I don't know of my Diantha's past? I do, Kate. Diantha has been very bad, but she will do better with me, in future. And I do love her."

Ashington said nothing to this amazing announcement, only raised one eyebrow in Diantha's direction.

"You needn't look so surprised, Ash," Diantha said hotly. "I *am* going to marry Henri! I love him, you see." She looked thoughtful, then shrugged. "I don't know quite how it happened, but there you are! Life is full of surprises. Oh, I know we shall be poor, but I have been thinking . . . could I not sell the jewels Ashington gave me, Henri? They would keep us for quite some time, I daresay."

At this, Ashington's sense of the absurd came to the forefront and he grinned wryly. "By all means, Di. Sell them with my good wishes," he said, and turned to Henri. "My felicitations, sir. You are, indeed, the luckiest of men."

Henri bowed. "*Merci,* my lord." He shot a glance at his sister and added slyly, "May I be the first to offer you *my* congratulations?"

The room was suddenly silent. Ashington scowled and turned away from Henri; Katherine's mouth trembled, and she busied herself with her reticule, opening and closing it aimlessly. Henri frowned and made as if to speak, but Honoria stepped into the breach.

"Well, this has all been very entertaining," she said, "but I believe that Kate has had quite enough excitement for one day. Come along, Kate, we'll go home now."

"My sister shall come with me," said Henri sternly. "Maman is waiting for us."

Diantha looked searchingly at Ashington, then laid her hand upon Henri's arm. "Perhaps it would be better if Kate were to go with Lady Basingstoke and Freddy," she said. "Your mother will have quite enough to deal with when she learns of our betrothal. Tomorrow will be time enough to fetch Kate." Henri seemed inclined to argue, but Diantha increased the pressure on his arm and shook her head, the tiniest of movements.

"Diantha is quite right," said Freddy briskly. He placed Katherine's bonnet tenderly on her head. "No, no, don't argue with me," he said. "Honoria is no doubt dying of curiosity, are you not, Aunt? It would be too cruel to deprive her of the opportunity to ask us embarrassing questions." He was rewarded with a weak smile, and he tucked Katherine's arm into his own. "We'll take the curricle," he said. "Ashington can find his own way home." He turned to Ashington. "I suppose I may rely on you to deal with him?" he said, his tone carefully even as he indicated Keswick, who was still stretched out on the floor.

"Assuredly," said Ashington. "Most assuredly."

"Very well, then," said Freddy. He opened the door for Katherine. "Come along, Kate." As Kate and

Freddy left the room, Lady Honoria Basingstoke turned back for a moment. "Do try not to be a fool, Ashington," she said coolly, and she was gone.

CHAPTER FOURTEEN

KATHERINE SHOOK HER HEAD. "No, Freddy. I'm going home today." She slumped lower into the depths of the wing chair in the corner. "It's pointless to discuss it any further."

"Kate, he'll come," Freddy said. "I know he will."

"Lord Ashington made his feelings quite clear yesterday," Katherine said; she could not quite manage to keep the bitterness out of her tone. "He won't come, and I won't wait."

"Kate's quite right," Honoria said from her side of the drawing room. "She'd be a fool to wait for Ashington."

Freddy turned to glare at his aunt, but Honoria surprised him by winking broadly. "Yes, Kate would be most unwise to expect anything from his lordship," Honoria continued. "Ashington is insufferably proud; he always has been, and I doubt very much if we may expect any lessening of his conceit at this late date."

"He has good reason to be proud," Katherine said hotly. "He is from one of the foremost families in England, you know." Freddy turned away; Honoria, older and wiser in the ways of deceit, met Katherine's gaze blandly. "I—I quite understand why Ashington wants nothing further to do with me," Katherine continued, her expression woebegone where it had been defiant. "He must think of his—his responsibilities, and his name and—and all that sort of thing," she finished weakly.

"Quite," said Honoria, and turned her attention back to the newspaper she had been reading. "There's an interesting item here," she said, tapping the paper with her finger. "In one of those dreadful columns that purport to relate the doings of the ton. It says—" she cleared her throat "—'A certain Lord K has departed quite suddenly for the Continent. His many friends and acquaintances hope that the climate there will prove salubrious, both to his health and his pocketbook.' Can you imagine the cheek? Not that Keswick doesn't deserve it, of course, but still…"

Katherine flushed, and gratefully turned her attention to Croaker, who was just entering the room.

"A Mr. L'Ecusson, madam, and Lady Blandford," said the butler. "Also," he added, his brow furrowed, "also a Monsoor Forcat."

Honoria waved her hand and the disapproving servant left to usher in the latest callers.

Diantha came in and swooped down on Katherine. "Oh, Kate," she said, hugging her betrothed's sister. "The greatest news!"

Katherine mustered up a smile. "My mother blessed your betrothal?" she suggested.

Diantha wrinkled her nose. "Not just at first," she admitted. "I think she was a trifle taken aback by my reputation. But once I explained to her my plan to sell Ashington's jewels to support us all, she seemed to warm to me. Though I must admit, I don't understand why she thought my scheme so funny."

"Maman has ever been ready to see the comical aspect of things," Henri said solemnly. "Wouldn't you agree, *ma soeur?*" His eyes twinkled.

"Oh, yes," Katherine said.

"At any rate," Diantha said, "we shall be married very soon. And, oh, Kate, we shan't be poor after all; in fact, we shall be quite rich!"

"Not rich, *madame la comtesse,*" Etienne Forcat said, "but rather, comfortable." He crossed the room to bow before Katherine. "Mademoiselle L'Ecusson," he said, bowing over her hand. "I am so delighted to meet you at last. You have led me a merry chase, you and your family, but...what is the saying? All is well that finishes well, *non?*"

Katherine was looking back and forth between Maître Forcat and her brother. "Henri?" she said, puzzled.

"It is...*incroyable,* Kate," Henri said, unable to hide his excitement. "Maître Forcat came from France to find us. It seems that I am the last male left alive in Maman's family. No other Berceau survived the revolution." He shook his head. "I still can't believe it."

"Kate, Kate, I am to be a countess again!" Diantha burst out. "La Comtesse de Berceau, to be precise. Isn't it exciting? I shall be a double countess—I wonder if that has ever happened before?"

Katherine looked even more confused. Maître Forcat stepped into the breach. "Perhaps I may explain," he said. "His Royal Highness, Louis XVIII of France, has commissioned me to trace the survivors of those families most loyal to his during the late Revolution. Your Maman's family, mademoiselle, the Berceaus, served the royal family most valiantly. Unfortunately, they served to the last man. So I came to England to find your brother and to beseech him to return to France, to his proper lands and title."

"We shall be leaving as soon as Diantha and I are married," Henri said. "Maman is *aux anges,* of course; she says that she cannot wait to return to France and to show us her native land, Kate."

"Leaving?" Katherine repeated blankly. She blinked once or twice, then managed a smile. "Well!" she said, too brightly. "I daresay that I shall like France very much, once I become accustomed to it. The weather there is said to be very fine, is it not?"

"Indeed it is, Kate," Freddy said gently. "And I shall come to visit you often, very often. You may sponsor me there, cos, as I have sponsored you in London."

Katherine's smile was genuine as she looked up at her distant cousin. "It will be my very great pleasure, Freddy."

"Ahem." Croaker, with a butler's inborn love of drama, waited until the room was absolutely still, then said, "My Lord Ashington, my lady."

Lord Ashington entered the room to find himself the centre of attention, much to his chagrin. Honoria, amused, winked at him and nudged Freddy; Katherine looked steadily out a nearby window, as though Ashington had never come in, and Henri watched the peer with a grave question in his eyes. Only Diantha behaved in anything approaching a normal **way**.

"Oh, Ash, you'll never guess," she babbled. "I am to be a French *comtesse!* And it's all thanks to you."

Henri asked with some amusement, "Indeed, my love? And what of me?"

"Oh, but Henri, I never should have met you again if I hadn't been so wildly jealous of Kate," Diantha said. "And I never should have been jealous of her if it hadn't been for Ashington falling in love with her. So you see, 'tis really all Ashington's doing."

Ashington's eyes had flown to Katherine, sitting so quietly in her corner. "My dear," he said, as though Diantha had not spoken. He crossed to Katherine. "We must talk," he said.

"There is nothing to talk about, my lord," said Katherine, still not meeting his eyes. "I shall say my farewell to you now; I shall be leaving very soon for France, with my brother." Finally she looked up. She said, "Good—goodbye, my lord."

"Kate, you can't! I shan't let you leave..." Ashington stopped, aware that five people were listening avidly to his every word. "Come into the foyer with me for a moment." He held out a hand to her.

Katherine shook her head; tears trembled on her eyelashes. "To what end, my lord?" she asked. "'Twere best done quickly."

Ashington squared his shoulders and swallowed his pride. "Very well, then," he said. "I believe that I left you under a misapprehension yesterday. You thought that I objected to your relationship to Henri, did you not?" Katherine did not answer. "It wasn't that, dearest girl, believe me," Ashington said. "Oh, I don't deny that I was taken aback; surely you'll agree that I had the right to be a little surprised? But though I do not know Henri as well as I should wish to—" he smiled at the tailor "—he has always struck me, in our dealings together, as an honest and upright fellow."

Henri bowed from the waist and grinned. "You are too kind, monsieur," he said.

"Keswick was another matter, though," Ashington continued, his smile fading. "Keswick, whom I despise as I have never despised any other in my life! The knowledge that you are cousin to him shook me to the core." Ashington took a few agitated steps back and forth. "I thought about it all night, tossing and turning in my bed, before the truth finally struck me." He dropped to one knee before an astonished Katherine. "Kate, I love you," he said. "It matters not a whit to me whom you are kin to or where you grew up.

I haven't the least interest in your nationality or your family's pedigree; whether your brother is a *comte* or a tailor is all one to me. The only thing that I am sure of is what you are to me, love—everything. Everything that I care for most in the world is tied up in you." He took her hand. "Marry me, Kate," he said fiercely. "Marry me, and make me the happiest of men."

"Well, *chérie*, it appears that you were right," Henri whispered to Diantha. "You said he'd come round, and here he is."

"Did you doubt it?" Diantha said airily. "I knew it from the first moment I saw them together. They were made for each other!" Henri swallowed his laughter.

"Well, Kate? Will you have me?" Ashington smiled at Katherine. "Be kind, sweeting; don't leave me in suspense."

The tears which had trembled on Katherine's lashes now flowed, unheeded, down her cheeks. "I am... very sensible of the honour you've shown me," she said brokenly, "but I cannot marry you." Her head bowed. "I am not worthy."

"Balderdash," said Freddy loudly, startling everyone in the room. "Don't forget, Kate, you are the sister of a French *comte*. Am I not right, monsieur?"

Etienne Forcat nodded. "Quite right," he said. "With your birth, mademoiselle, you might look as high as you wish for a husband."

"The only question is," Freddy continued, "is Ashington worthy of you?"

"Probably not," said Ashington. "But I believe that Kate is great-hearted enough to forgive me my shortcomings. Aren't you, Kate?" He pressed a kiss onto the palm of her hand.

Katherine pulled her hand from Ashington's grasp. "Keswick would never let us be happy," she whispered. "If he were to learn that we were wed, he would come back and tell everyone...who I am. He hates you, my lord, and would never rest until he had ruined you, through me."

"But what is there to tell, Kate?" Freddy asked, spreading his hands wide. "All that Keswick may say to your detriment is that you are his cousin. A sad impediment, I grant you, but the fact that you are sister to a French *comte* and the much-loved wife of a peer will surely silence the most vicious of gossips."

"Very true," said Ashington. He smiled. "And should anyone be so unwise as to mention a certain tailor shop, I daresay that Freddy and Aunt Honoria will quickly put paid to that notion."

"We shall," said Honoria, a martial light gleaming in her eyes. "Indeed we shall!"

Katherine scanned Ashington's face anxiously. "Are you sure, Ash?" she asked. "Are you quite, quite sure?"

Lord Ashington could wait no longer. He swept Katherine to her feet and, before five pairs of staring eyes, pressed his lips to hers.

"Well," gasped Diantha. "They may have called me fast, but even I should never have dared to kiss a man in public."

"No?" retorted Henri with a wicked smile. Before Diantha could protest, he took her in his strong arms. "Prepare yourself, *ma chérie!*"

Freddy Basingstoke blushed beet-red. "Monsieur Forcat," he said hastily, "pray allow me to stand you to a brandy." He took the French solicitor's arm. "In the library." He led the solicitor out of the room. Honoria, bringing up the rear, cast one last look at the kissing couples. "Love!" she said with great disgust. "Bah!"

PENNY JORDAN

Sins and infidelities...
Dreams and obsessions...
Shattering secrets
unfold in...

THE HIDDEN YEARS

SAGE — stunning, sensual and vibrant, she spent a lifetime distancing herself from a past too painful to confront... the mother who seemed to hold her at bay, the father who resented her and the heartache of unfulfilled love. To the world, Sage was independent and invulnerable— but it was a mask she cultivated to hide a desperation she herself couldn't quite understand... until an unforeseen turn of events drew her into the discovery of the hidden years, finally allowing Sage to open her heart to a passion denied for so long.

The Hidden Years—a compelling novel of truth and passion that will unlock the heart and soul of every woman.

AVAILABLE IN OCTOBER!
Watch for your opportunity to complete your Penny Jordan set.
POWER PLAY and SILVER will also be available in October.

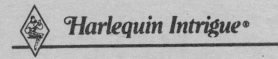

Harlequin Intrigue®

Trust No One...

When you are outwitting a cunning killer, confronting dark secrets or unmasking a devious imposter, it's hard to know whom to trust. Strong arms reach out to embrace you—but are they a safe harbor...or a tiger's den?

When you're on the run, do you dare to fall in love?

For heart-stopping suspense and heart-stirring romance, read Harlequin Intrigue. Two new titles each month.

HARLEQUIN INTRIGUE—where you can expect the unexpected.